H. RAM

Susan Daitch was born in 1954 in New Haven, Connecticut. She was educated at Barnard College in New York City (where she has been a guest faculty member in recent years) and the Whitney Museum Independent Study Program. Her first novel, *L.C.*, was published by Virago Press in England (1986) and by Harcourt, Brace in the U.S. (1987); it was also a selection of the Quality Paperback Book Club. Her second novel, *The Colorist*, was published by Vintage as a paperback original in 1990. Her shorter fiction has been anthologized in such books as *After Yesterday's Crash: The Avant-Pop Anthology, Transgressions: The Iowa Anthology of Experimental Fiction, Disorderly Conduct: the VLS Fiction Reader,* and *So Very English: A Serpent's Tail Compilation.* She has taught at Bennington College and at the Iowa Writers' Workshop, and since 1988 has been on the faculty of Sarah Lawrence College, Bronxville, New York. She lives in New York City with her son.

Also by Susan Daitch

L. C.

The Colorist

Storytown

stories by

Susan Daitch

Dalkey Archive Press

"Killer Whales" and "The Restorer" first appeared in the *Voice Literary Supplement,* "Fishwanda" in *So Very English,* ed. Susan Rowe (Serpent's Tail, 1991), "Aedicule" in the "Good-bye Columbus" issue of the *Literary Review,* "Doubling" in *One Meadway,* "Incunabula #1" in *Instant Classics,* "Incunabula #2" in *Central Park,* "Incunabula #3" in *Tourist Attractions* (Top Stories), "X ≠ Y" in *Bomb* and *Fiction International,* "On Habit" in *Documents,* and "Storytown" in *Lo Spazio Umano.* "Analogue" first appeared in a special issue of the *Iowa Review,* published simultaneously in book form as *Transgressions: The Iowa Anthology of Innovative Fiction,* ed. Lee Montgomery, Mary Hussmann, and David Hamilton (Univ. of Iowa Press, 1994). All of these stories have been revised for the present collection.

Library of Congress Cataloging-in-Publication Data
Daitch, Susan.
Storytown : stories / by Susan Daitch. — 1st ed.
        p.   cm.
1. Manners and customs—Fiction. I. Title.
PS3554.A33S76   1996   813'.54—dc20   95-26578
ISBN 1-56478-094-5

Partially funded by a grant from the Illinois Arts Council.

Dalkey Archive Press
Illinois State University
Campus Box 4241
Normal, IL 61790-4241

Printed on permanent/durable acid-free paper and bound in the United States of America.

Contents

Acknowledgments

FOR CRITICAL READINGS and discussions over the years these stories were written, special thanks to Esther Allen, Leslie Camhi, Lisa Cartwright, Linda Collins, Deirdre Summerbell, and especially John Foster, whose support has been invaluable. I am also grateful to Andrea Kahn who helped with architectural questions from aedicules to spatial habits, Karen Weltman (companion in Storytown) and Jon Sterngass, Carol Anne Klonarides and Michael Owen, Laura Cottingham, Jennifer Gordon for her translation of "Analogue," which added the Napoleonic concept of a house divided by divorce, and my sisters Cheryl and Amy for their comic interventions at the best possible moments.

Killer Whales

I woke up to find Gregor Samsa in my sink. He was enormous, at least two inches long, blue-black, and very fast. I grabbed a china teacup, something the last tenant had left in the house, placed it over him, and slid the covered bug to a position over the drain. I hoped he would figure that crawling down the hole was his only alternative, although his scutcheoned shell was far too broad to allow him to do so easily. He was a real monster, and I expected the teacup itself might move across the stainless steel any minute, its rim scraping the leftover grit of cleanser and coffee grounds. It was raining into the bay, rain streaked the kitchen window and ran into pots of baby cacti and pansies that a catalogue had promised would grow to sequoia dimensions. I opened the window and let it rain in. The spigots and faucets were soon dotted with tiny convex reflections. My beetle under china roses slumbered.

The wind dropped, and the rain fell straight down so that a haze of water bounced from shingles. Gutters turned riverlike and drainpipes led to miniature versions of Niagara Falls. I walked out into the rain, stood beside a laurel tree, and looked into my neighbor's window. He had changed the arrangement of figures set out behind small panes of glass, and I was glad because I hadn't seen him for a while. A statue of Saint Francis faced outward from the sill, arms outstretched, one hand chipped off, white plaster showing through the scratched brown paint of his robe. He was surrounded by toy sheep, soldiers, a couple of windup Godzillas, a toy bed with two syringes tucked in it, and a candlestick which had a flame-shaped light bulb where a wick would have been. I hadn't seen these objects before. I was afraid my neighbor would catch me staring at the sleeping needles as water dripped down my back, but his ground-floor apartment looked empty. Behind a louvered glass door the rooms were dim, tables dusty.

SOME THINGS aren't as different as people like to claim. When I was a child I used to think about language as an odd job lot of words, random and haphazard, you find a string to do the work, to effect meaning. Then the metaphor evolved again. Words were like a school of jellyfish with thousands of tentacles streaming below the surface, and some of those tentacles were attached or stuck together below the waves: the seemingly unconnected jellyfish were really Siamese twins if you looked closely. The connections might be syllables or synonyms. I was a rubberized underwater diver looking for those strands which tied words together. How might *Aztec* be like *Creole* or *Yayoi* like *Ikan?* I don't think I was innocently looking for natural linguistic connections— I deliberately tied tentacles together, ignoring my own stung fingers. Abandoning articulate speech, I turned to origins: I listened to babies, trying to determine when a child begins to drop the nonsense from his or her speech and link the production of sounds to the expression of desire, gratification, or frustration. Crawling, staring, drooling onto tape recorders, they slowly begin to identify clusters of sounds, priming the language pump, it's called. For several years I watched them play and cry, then shifted my attention to unlocking the meaning of monkey chatter and bird songs. I monitored whale calls, seismographic blurps on a blue screen, interpreting each wave as if it were a kind of dangling clause or tense shift, yet often felt lost in the proto-languages of animals and children.

Now I look at words as isolated catatonic patients in a state hospital whose funds have been cut off. It is a scene of bankruptcy where there is no longer any relationship between sound and meaning. The orderlies smoke joints in the unswept halls and take all kinds of pills right out in the chaotic open. They speak of morphine in morphemes, if possible, and I'm even more convinced of the futility of this project, looking for sources.

I WORK AT the university lab annotating the speech of sea animals, particularly the killer whales on loan from Sea World in San Diego. The lab, crescent-shaped, a fingernail clipping in the sand, is underground, equipment separated by plates of glass from huge tanks which contain the animals, and I watch them swim in very blue water. If the animals can see me, through windows on the inner curve, they give no sign. There are manatees, members of the Siren family, and a tank of rare pygmy sperm whales. Black-and-white killer whales are really giant porpoises; they're fast swimmers, able to swallow dolphins and smaller porpoises alive. According to Eskimo legends, killer whales began as hungry wolves who transformed themselves into aquatic creatures, overwhelmed by the seduction of hunting in the Pacific, and once transformed, none of them returned to land. Ferocious in packs, they are known to eat the weak and wounded members of their own families, but in Sea World or here in the lab, there's hardly a chance for cannibalism. In Sea World they performed with swimmers on school vacation; girls held up rings for them to catch at the end of their noses. In enclosed pools the porpoises were fed small live fish, easily caught, no pursuit involved; they consumed meals with the matter-of-fact languor of someone on a couch tossing popcorn into his mouth.

The young imitated and learned their mothers' calls, but the question was posed: If one of the mothers died, would the calf remember her call or would it learn the adopted call of some other killer whale? I threw them fish and listened closely, but all our mothers lived, and mimesis continued without interruption. I would pat the whales when they surfaced, and felt something had been added to my identity when they recognized me. Sea World knew our lab was waiting for the possibility of observing the effect of a parent's death on learning calls, but it wasn't an experiment we could perform. In Sea World when a mother died on its own of more or less natural causes, the calf was transferred up north to our lab.

I watched them swim and dive in bluish light and listened to their calls. The patterns of their swimming followed similar curves traced by the device that records their speech, but I wondered if the orphan calf, as she mimicked the chain of sounds produced by some other member of the herd, was able to forget her mother in the middle of an untroubled swim. Did she hear echoes of her mother's call mixed up in another whale's bark? These were questions for electrodes and heart monitors. Her face is smooth, teeth glinted. I was clueless.

Once my neighbor put a fishbowl in his window. Goldfish and guppies swam through a miniature pink castle surrounded by artificial ferns. A naked Barbie doll, or something like one, sat on the sill watching the fish. The doll's knees weren't jointed, so its legs shot straight out, aggressively. On the other side of the broad window ledge another doll was submerged head down in a glass tank, surrounded by rubber fish placed in inquisitive attitudes as if they were watching her, although later it occurred to me the rubber fish setup might have been an ambush. The doll's legs stuck out above the rim and its blonde hair floated in the water. I'm not sure if this was a gesture in my direction, a way of beckoning, teasing, or mimicking, and I never asked. Perhaps the tableau had nothing to do with me at all. Up until then the sill had contained a collection of cigarette lighters shaped like pistols, and a lamp whose base was an Elvis Presley head. I'd thought my neighbor had an interest in things which model themselves after something else, which hide behind another identity or another history, but now I'm not so sure. The last time I saw him he had become very thin and walked slowly, stopping to buy a newspaper at our corner. My neighbor who constructs stories out of ephemera—toys, needles, and nicked-up saints—is dying, and I don't know if there's been anyone in to learn his speech, anyone who could decode those window displays, and say with certainty, *this is what he meant by . . . and I will repeat to you. . . .* I called him before I left, but no one picked up. The light changed slightly over the water, although I couldn't see the sky, but without looking at a clock I knew it was late, locked up the lab, and began to drive away from the coast.

FOUR ALL-NIGHTERS huddled together, a lit island in a dark street: 24-hour Bus Stop Fruit and Vegetables with a marquee constructed of lemons, peaches, and eggplant stacked outside; That's Rentertainment, a video store whose windows displayed life-size cardboard cutouts of muscled actors and animated caricatures that too seemed to glow in the dark; a gas station defended by looping elephantine hoses; and a Greek restaurant. I thought I might see the same people at each, buying eggplant, renting a movie, sitting in the restaurant drinking coffee to stay awake, then driving home.

Electric lights shaped like candles had been placed in each of Demeter's windows, romantic in the rain if you've just driven up for gas and aren't anxious to get home. I parked, seduced by the electric candles, but also because Demeter's aluminum-sided diner reminded me of Sam's, torn down long ago in another city. I used to take a bus from school to Sam's downtown, sitting with friends at a curving formica counter with boomerang shapes embedded in it; we'd order Cokes. The man who fried everything under the sun had a thin, pissed-off face. We watched him. However much we tried to wrinkle our gray skirts and green blazers, we felt trapped and ordinary, while his tattoo of a woman with a whip and dangling cigarette spoke of foreignness. I was sure he hated us because we ordered little more than french fries and showed no visible signs of responsibility. Sam's had an electric sign over the grill. Above the name of the restaurant was a blackboard-colored field split by a hyperbolic curve with a dot of light tracing its trajectory. The spellbinding illusion was that the color of the dot of light changed as it traveled along the curve. Blue hill, green valley, yellow hill, red valley, purple hill, then back to the beginning, a visual metronome. It was mesmerizing when you had nothing to talk about, or even when you did.

The bathroom in Sam's reflected someone's idea of what signified feminine: smudged gray and pink tile, cracked formica threatening to spill its gold glitter. But the feminine was covered by names and numbers scratched into yellow metal, written on walls and mirrors, even the paper towel dispenser: pleadings and demands, secrets made public, ridiculous limericks. The Aztecs and Mayans had chalk talk, pictogramic calendars or talking pictures, and I wondered if the names in Sam's bathroom weren't some kind of message system too. I didn't imagine the rude poems and crooked hearts had anything to do with loneliness. They were just dirty and funny. I saw men and women meet each other at Sam's. They slid into booths, or sat down heavily, somehow they found each other. I tried to listen to their conversations, but from the counter I couldn't really hear anything. Once I heard the phrase *dirty laundry,* several times the word *telephone,* then *letter from Plei-ku.*

We were warned not to go there. The nail in the coffin of our trips to Sam's came when a man was arrested in one of the booths. I don't remember what he was charged with or if he was convicted, but I continued to go there, usually alone. I would have given anything for a weekend job at Sea World swimming with the porpoises, but we lived in a landlocked state. In a small town near two state lines Sam's served as amusement park and laboratory. I saw packages left in the phone booth whose wooden door, an accordion of two panels, easily offered a screen. Women came and went quickly in the late afternoon, not stopping to talk to each other in booths or over the counter. The long-haired men who picked up the packages used the word *babe,* like nothing I'd ever heard before.

My mother's warnings hadn't described them. Her language was so full of omissions that I didn't learn it. I've read of tribes where one language is spoken by men and a quite different one by women, but consider a tribe in which daughters speak a separate language, unrelated to that of their mothers—an impractical invention, ridiculous and fantastic. Let's say they do speak the same language, but in this tribe the language is constructed so that mothers and daughters who take pleasure in contradicting each other are able to do so at every possible opportunity. Every time a spear is hammered, every time a bowl is cast, or fish are fried, they disagree. One says something is blue, the other says no, it's green, one says offense is taken, the other says no, you misinterpret, you always do, and I'm sick of it. The tanks I watch appear serene in comparison; one learns the calls of the other, and that's it. I have no one to repeat my mother's warnings to in any case, except possibly baby killer whales who ignore me, just as a child who is too often told what to do might finally ignore an adult, or try to, so perhaps the result is the same.

AT DEMETER'S the news on the hour is broadcast from a radio kept by the cash register. Mr. Demeter turns it on only late at night when a few drivers or midnight video renters straggle in, and the diner is sporadically empty anyway. The announcer snaps out the words *Persian Gulf.* It's difficult to pronounce these soft syllables with such brittleness. *Pershun. Per-son.*

Sand as fine as powdered sugar, Mr. Demeter echoed something he once heard.

The radio again: *Tariq, Kerkuk, Baghdad, Mesopotamia,* and *Al Basra* slam into *typhus, typhoid, microorganisms.* Here the tongue lingers. I try to imitate the announcer but am unable to mimic his speech. *Forty thousand body bags have just been ordered, although no shot has yet been fired.* Demeter hits the cash register so ringing interrupts the newscast. He's not really successful in blocking out the sound, and I imagine if Bartleby suffered paralysis as a result of working in a dead letter office, those who sew and measure zippers and nylon on a body bag assembly line may also linger in future cells saying only *I prefer not to.* No one will guess their histories. I line up the salt and pepper shakers, the sugar dispenser, and the ketchup bottle as if each object represents a sewing machine operator, a packer, a filer of invoices. Windows are streaked with rain, and within That's Rentertainment a clerk is counting orange Video Bucks, another moves a cardboard Julia Roberts out of the window, putting his hands between her legs to lift her and laughing at a man who stares at him, laughing too. Plastic coverings are lowered over fruit and vegetables next door. Under blinking fluorescent lights, daffodils, hyacinths, and paper whites glow like supernatural parodies of themselves.

SOMEONE HAD wiped dust from the jalousied door. Objects had been removed from his window, and it remained empty the next day as well. Just a week before the monster had risen from my drain. Perhaps Gregor Samsa fled with the instinctive knowledge that everything he was used to had been slated to be swept away. I turned on the television, but these kinds of deaths aren't reported, there are so many of them. Even after the news I left it on, providing a blur of sound in the house for a few minutes. I didn't pay attention really, but as something like *America's Most Wanted* or *Unsolved Mysteries* followed the news broadcast it occurred to me that the man behind the grill at Sam's might turn up on one of these programs, computer aged, because it's years later. All kinds of people do, followed by the warning: *If you should see this man or woman, please call. . . .* If this should happen, my mother will say, I told you so, you were lucky to get away unharmed. Perhaps I know her language better than I realize or am ever willing to admit.

THE KILLER whales swim in confined pools. Curves of whale speech snaking across a laboratory monitor resemble the curve of the electric sign in Sam's that held you spellbound, *Drink Coke, Drink Coke, Drink Coke.* I recognize patterns of sound, but the meanings they bark remain elusive. Whether they are arguing or talking about dinner, expressing boredom or depression, the screen doesn't tell me, but I sit and watch. It's late. At Demeter's Mr. D has refused to listen to the radio for the time being, he doesn't want to hear about refugees or nerve gas, so I get a coffee to go and return to work for a few more hours. The microphones are set in the whale pool. I am listening.

The Restorer

H E HELD A PIPE to the boy's mouth so he could try to smoke. Another child, a girl, stared straight at Anne. She touched the boy's shirt as he sucked on the pipe stem, running her hand down his sleeve, then she took a step back. The room was crowded with people, and all of them, in their own way, looked as if they were having a good time. A woman, dress half-untied, held her glass out for more, and a man, grinning, poured a stream of red wine into it. He must have been standing on a box or a chair because he was unnaturally higher than the rest. One musician played some kind of instrument Anne couldn't identify, and he, too, looked straight at her. A red parrot standing on his perch in the corner seemed the only thing not smiling, even the dog was. Anne went next door to borrow a ruler. The stream of wine had fallen in a perfect perpendicular. When she returned she held the straight edge up to it, and with a careful stroke reddened the streak of color which had begun to darken and crackle.

Red triangle: the woman's glass at the center of the painting was sharp and had resisted aging. She was afraid to touch the untidy woman having her glass filled. A shadow fell across her features, and the paint was badly cracked. Anne cleaned her face with spit, but it remained eclipsed and brittle-looking. She lined up her narrowest sable brushes— the last seemed to contain only two or three hairs—but now her hand stopped within an inch of her face. It was too fragile. Nearby the expression of the man who offered the boy a smoke appeared lewd and distorted. She put her nose up to his. No one was watching. She was alone in her studio. Out the painted window lay The Hague or Rotterdam. A tag attached to its lower left corner read *Merry Company,* Jan Steen (1626-1679). She turned *Merry Company* against the wall.

AT MIDDAY two art handlers walked in carrying *Women of Algiers in Their Room.* They entered without knocking, set the painting down where Anne indicated, then left, stuffing white gloves into their back pockets. She stood very close to the canvas, put her finger in her mouth, then rubbed a woman's calf with spit. Her wet finger traced the bronze armband of their African slave and the loops of a hookah sitting beside a pair of empty shoes, tossed aside and neglected. Dirt and dust came off on her hands. Their skin was especially cracked; pigment splintered and fractured. She squeezed a blob of antiseptic titanium white onto a glass plate, then added a smudge of rose, but the result turned rubber doll pink. On another part of the glass Anne blended the skin color she imagined Delacroix had originally used and in the third corner the aged, yellowed flesh that remained. Were the Algerians supposed to be light rose-colored women? Anne squeezed burnt sienna onto the plate but left it lying inert and unmixed. She had to follow the pinkish dictates of his original intentions. Their attendant, grown blurred and sketchy, looked as if she were visiting from another picture, twentieth century. Either he had deliberately painted this woman vague and blocky, or her dimmed face was the result of conscious overpainting by some other restorer who had worked anonymously in some other city, sometime between Delacroix and Anne.

HER STUDIO was in a sub-basement. It had two doors; one was huge, chipped gray, split into two horizontal halves. That was the freight elevator, used to deliver and retrieve paintings. The pictures came from all over the world, unless they were too fragile or too valuable, then she had to go to them. Her pockets were full of métro stubs and taxi receipts.

REMBRANDT SEARED by acid in Kassel; *Guernica* splattered with red paint during the Vietnam war; Velásquez cut to ribbons in London after World War I; Correggio's erotic *Leda* decapitated in 1726 by a duc d'Orleans whose confessor had persuaded him of the painting's corrupting influence. It was later stolen by Napoleon, and the head repainted. By the time Anne saw *Leda* in Rome there was little she could do. The new head had been painted thickly, with no trace of an attempt to imitate Correggio's style. It would have been like repairing a newspaper cartoon whose image crumbles in your hands, Anne told them. A copy of the painting was said to have been made in Prague before *Leda* was chopped up, but no one in Rome had ever seen the replica. A soldier who had been loyal to Mussolini returned from the east carrying a rumor of its existence. The copy might still be in Prague or it might not be, the Italians shrugged. Back in her sub-basement Anne drew swan feathers on scraps of paper or the lid of a pizza box lying near the telephone: feathers between legs, the way Correggio might have drawn them.

In Kassel the man who flung corrosives made statements to the effect that he felt mistreated and wanted to destroy an object representative of authority. He could have held a human hostage (from Volkswagen, Krupp, I. M. Farben), but he chose a quick squirt at Rembrandt, Rubens, Cranach the Elder, and Klee. Anne often didn't know whose side to take, when the slashes, acid, and red paint seemed inseparable from the canvas, and she wanted to just grab a cab back to the airport. During the Kassel restoration she was taken as a respected guest to an expensive restaurant. Sitting on her hands she couldn't decide what to order in a language she didn't understand, but in a sudden moment of resolve, she argued for doing nothing to repair the damage even though it was in her interest to continue the work. Later, standing in the women's room, she combed her hair until it flattened out like grass someone had sat on for a long time and wondered if her hosts secretly thought she was some kind of relic herself. Returning to the table she continued to urge that wrinkles and scars be retained. No face-lifts, no cosmetic surgery. The marks were now part of the picture's history and ought to be preserved as well.

Grasping a warm scotch in one hand, a deeply tanned man seated to her left made a remark about the sex of oysters. Male, female, hermaphrodite, you don't know until you open the shell, he said, holding his glass as if it were the key to the city. He looked at her as he spoke, and Anne wondered if he were making a comment about herself, with her rumpled suit and broken nails. It seemed to her that his offhand glance was a way of saying you and your ideas are ridiculous. The combination of wine and well-dressed old men was putting her to sleep, so she ignored him, staring out the window while they waited for the check, pinching herself awake, wondering if she rolled her eyes when he said *open the shell.* A boy walked by wearing sunglasses (although it was night) and singing loudly, but the only words Anne could make out sounded like "poodle brains." A truck rolled past, a fish wearing a beret and smoking a cigar painted on its side. Anne thought about cheap paint slapped onto the side of a metal truck. It would peel off in no time. For such materials there was no hope. The images would disappear in a blink.

SMASHED WHILE squads of men and dogs looked for a cache of drugs or smuggled state secrets. These were depressing jobs. Anne could understand how a spectator might feel canvas eyes staring at him or her and have to do something to make the staring stop. The damage done by the dispossessed or psychotic was one thing, but the damage of the FBI, CIA, and Interpol was something else. She usually referred these jobs to another restorer. Anne wondered if this was a false position because she would otherwise do any job that came through the double doors. She had nothing against the Rockefellers, Japanese insurance companies, or whoever owned the objects she worked on. She had no religious or ideological ax to grind. Despite her hesitation she negated the effects of those who did.

TELEVISION. Extreme desecration can lead to a kind of celebrity conferred on the vandal, and the restorer becomes an authority, in turn. Anne had been called to go on television once. Makeup artists fluttered around her, their corned beef sandwiches from the studio cafeteria left half eaten next to pressed powders of all skin colors. They asked if she was nervous, but she remained calm and distanced from the camera as if it were just another piece of furniture. She explained what she did, she referred to job X and job Y, responded familiarly to the man interviewing her, using his first name. Her calmness was displaced when the man who slashed the Metropolitan's Vermeer was broadcast via satellite. She felt somber and prosaic in comparison. His contorted speech was eloquent and controversial. Before they cut him off he made analogies between corroded arteries and career criminals, between toasters and time bombs. Even the branches of his metaphors were symbolic on their own apart from the relationship he proposed in the comparison. He was said to have been very repentant and, like the subway vigilante who shot several people, wanted to turn back the clock and allow the rents he caused to melt away. Anne had first seen the man on the news after the story about American soldiers landing in Honduras and before the exclusive interview with the boy who claimed he murdered his sleeping girlfriend in self-defense. His static image had flashed across the television she kept in the studio, its screen wedged between Klee and a Pollock, the most difficult of all when paint starts to flake.

THE SUB-BASEMENT was a thick walled cell immune from vandals and most catastrophes. It was a hospital, a cultural auto/ body shop. Black telephone, radio, Hellenic coffee cups, Chinese takeout cartons, and pizza boxes still holding cold slices. Paint in tubes and jars, color swatches, books on chemistry, row after row of colors in various forms, dry and wet.

A CRATE OF Pissarros, untouched since 1914. German soldiers had wiped their boots on paintings found in his studio in Louveciennes. Anne carefully scraped real mud and tried to match the color of painted dirt. A row of windows looked beyond repair. He advised his son Lucien to favor caricature rather than prettiness. Which Lucien chose, Anne didn't know. Yellow was, for Whistler, a happy color, Lucien wrote back from England. His father gave up the apartment in Paris, gave up trips to visit his son. He kept hoping to be paid for his work; he projected sales and income and was constantly disappointed. Critics accused him of sick eyes, suffering from the illness of those who see only blue, and he quoted the notices to his son. When she read *sick eyes,* Anne imagined a man reeling around Brittany wearing 3-D glasses, or a cartoon figure with an idiot's grin plastered to his face who walked the streets, hair stuck together in paint-smeared clumps much like hers. Anne knew she was paid more to mend the cracks in Pissarro's painted rooftops than he had received for a whole collection of pictures. Six months after his death, his dealer, Durand-Ruel, sold his paintings for 10,000 to 20,000 francs each.

When Pissarro was afraid of looking at canvases he turned them against the wall. Anne's studio was full of stained, yellowed backs; dirty and reproachful echoes of what lay on the reverse. He wrote to his son that he had always thought them precious gems but feared they had turned into monsters.

ARRIVING FROM Paris, another crate. She was a waitress working in Le Lapin Agile, serving Apollinaire and Jarry. Picasso takes a cigarette wrapper from her hand when she tries to clear the table. His hands are dry and squarish. She wishes she had saved the bit of paper. It would be worth a fortune. The owner will say she hasn't done her job, *Look at the mess you've left.* She gulps a brandy when his back is turned. Apollinaire winks at her. Anne carefully opened the crate with a hammer, yet as she did so packing excelsior spilled out all over the floor. A blue Gauloise wrapper stuck out of the wooden fluff. Had it fallen off the original painting or had one of the art handlers carelessly stuffed it in the packing? The cellophane was still bound to the wrapper. The blue was too bright. It was new.

UNDER A SELF-portrait, another face emerged. Anne checked the accompanying papers, tossing aside excelsior and pieces of packing tape. There was no mention of underpainting. As she cleaned Courbet's cheek, a second pair of eyes, a nose, and a mouth appeared. She studied the second face, referred to some books, ran up to the museum gift shop, bought some postcards, and held the color reproductions up to the (two) originals. An eyelid, a shadowy wisp of a comma, could be made out just under the lower lashes of the other; a nose poked through beside the mouth, mimicking the more visible one. Anne's mouth grew dry. She stopped cleaning. Like Siamese twins with one heart or one liver, one could be saved, but the other had to be destroyed. Together they were a freak, a restorer's nightmare of palimpsest. The first layer of paint could be easily wiped away, or she could restore the self-portrait and obliterate the other. No one would know. She was the only witness, but she was curious about the character of the underpainting. Who was buried there? In facing a vendetta of pigment, mute and still causing big problems, Anne turned on her television. Women who wore provocative clothes sat on a stage along with their husbands or boyfriends. They giggled and defended their clothing, then their partners came forward and threw cut-up shorts and transparent dresses into the audience. *Help me get rid of these, will you?* The audience laughed and applauded. Anne watched for a while, then switched off the talk show and left her studio, locking the door behind her.

The museum basement and sub-basement were filled with workers packing and filing. West Indian carpenters built sculpture stands, reggae leaked from their Walkmans; temps stapled invoices; young men and women carried books and reproductions up to other floors. They fascinated Anne. Sometimes their hair looked wet in the morning, and their clothes were often wrinkled or secondhand. The large suits and beaded sweaters may have belonged to fathers and mothers who could no longer imagine why anyone would want to wear the clothing of the postwar era they had saved for no reason. The young museum workers grew up in houses with attics, cellars covered over with knotty pine paneling, garages full of stored, nearly discarded things hanging from rafters like bats constructed from aggregates of sports equipment and car parts. Now they lived in railroad walk-ups furnished with the marginalia of suburban life. Pool tables or outdoor grills might molder away, untransferable to narrow urban living spaces, but bar stools and floor lamps shaped like question marks found new homes. Anne herself had grown up in such a house but neither retrieved nor salvaged anything from it. She knew a few of them by their first names, and they were surprised to see her out during lunch hour. Usually she had food delivered.

Perhaps the artist had been so infatuated with the subject of the earlier portrait that the likeness had been unbearable, and in an act of either narcissism or longing, he covered it over with a portrait of himself. On the other hand an obsession grounded in fear and loathing might have grabbed him by the lapels, and so the only way he could shake himself free was to paint over the thing. Either way, it was an uncanny image, an amalgam of body parts and jumbled gazes. Upstairs in the museum gift shop Anne spun racks of postcards, as if in the sheer multiplicity of images the identity of the earlier portrait might be revealed. What did it mean to look at a photograph, for example, so long it finally dissolved into the flat thing it really was? Anne remembered she had spent a lot of time looking at pictures of John Lennon in 1966. She eventually threw the pictures away and left home. She wished she had them now, not out of nostalgia, but because remembering what she had thought, even stupidly, of John Lennon might shed some light on her dilemma. She rarely saw Central Park during the day but walked into it because she found herself outside the museum and didn't know where else to go.

ANNE RETURNED to the mutilated Pissarros. She wanted to paint figures in the empty windows. She had to restrain herself from painting a smiley face somewhere in the Delacroix. She made a small paper airplane out of the accidental cigarette wrapper.

There was a knock on the door. Delivery, Szechuan baby shrimp with oyster sauce. Anne didn't know if the face underneath was male or female. She guessed it was a woman, but her guess was wobbly and uncertain. She let the rice turn cold, a grainy white brick, then stuck chopsticks into the carton and drew a face on it so the thing looked like a bug.

HE KNOCKED on the door as if he were a delivery boy who wasn't sure he had the right address and would rather be on a subway reading advertisements to himself. He had heard there were problems with the cleaning and restoration of the portrait. Later Anne would remember he hadn't said which one, but she assumed he meant the project she was working on. How did he know about it? It was possible a lost child who wandered into her studio by mistake had told someone upstairs about a picture with four eyes, but playing dumb, Anne asked him what he was talking about. He insisted there had been letters, and that Anne had been dawdling over the painting for months. No one had seen it, and letters had gone unanswered.

"What's the problem? Can I see the painting, please?"

She thought she knew all the curators but had never seen this man before. He looked vaguely familiar, but she wasn't sure. She stared at the long space between his nose and his upper lip that gave him an imperious air, but at the same time made him resemble a rabbit. His navy blue suit, which might have been snitched from a shopwindow, didn't quite fit. His wrists hung out below the sleeves, and his tie was wrinkled, but his manner was officious. Anne remembered one night while walking home she'd been easily conned out of twenty dollars. A stranger had approached her on a deserted street, one lined with restaurant back doors and cardboard warrens. Although empty at the time, it was often traveled as a kind of exit ramp connected to one of the broader avenues. He stood very close to Anne and floated a story about being locked out of a car or an apartment. As the man became increasingly agitated, she handed him the money. Anne felt just as cornered now and overly conscious of the sound of teenage children confronting their abusive potential stepfathers on the television. *Don't marry him, Mom!* She turned the painting around.

SPECIAL PHOTOGRAPHERS were called in. The painting was X-rayed. It was on the front page of several newspapers, but none of the photographers or radiographs solved the problem, and no one was able to decide what to do with the double portraits. The canvas stood like a freak in the center of Anne's sub-basement studio. Although she refused to touch the painting, he kept visiting her, and there was nothing she could do to make him leave. When she heard his polite knocking she wanted to scream. Because he somehow sensed that he was irritating, he brought her grape leaves from the Greek place on Madison Avenue and half carafes of wine from the restaurant upstairs, as if gifts would appease her. Anne was only more insulted. She asked him to wipe his hands on paper towels before he touched anything. It was the only thing she could make him do. Sometimes he brought a book and sat in a chair so she felt guilty about turning on the television while she worked. Despite his attentions he really was oblivious to her once he arrived. She'd never asked his name since she believed she was supposed to have known it, but then couldn't check the museum's directory. Anne began to doubt whether he worked in the museum at all and wondered if he were some crank trustee who had a secret investment in the painting and its notoriety. Sometimes his accent slipped into the language of streets, not the streets adjacent to the museum, and when he did it was clear he hadn't, like the others, come from houses with large amounts of storage space. *Listen here. You know what I'm saying to you?* But even that inflected voice could have been a put-on. She didn't know who he was. She wanted to throttle him.

The X rays were inconclusive as to the identity or even the gender of the portrait underneath. Anne tacked up a row of them as if her studio were an oncologist's office and she was watching the progress of a cluster of cancer cells. Meetings were held, but still no decisions were made about the picture.

One night, while Anne was working late, he knocked on her door.

Are you a felon, or what? Should I be afraid of you? What are you doing here?

She turned up her television to signify that she was very busy, and he should go home. Sensing this, he said he had nothing to do and just wanted to look at the X rays. Also he had a request to make. Anne's eyebrows reached to the vaulted ceiling.

"You have a request to make? Who do you think you are?"

"I've come to ask you to remove the later self-portrait entirely. Plenty of photographs have been taken of it. There are postcards of the self-portrait upstairs. Everyone is familiar with the image. It's been on the cover of books." He twisted one of the buttons on his shirt. "It's had a good run," he continued. "It's the right thing to do. The picture underneath should be revealed and preserved. Think of yourself as an archeologist uncovering the original foundation. You've begun a job, OK, let's finish it off."

She told him she knew what was up. Naively she thought sympathy might disarm him.

"You stare at a painting for a long time, and you begin to want to do things to it." (The smiley faces, the figures added to windows, wiping away Dutch bourgeois grins.) "The painting seems overwhelming, and you want to take revenge. Looking is too ordinary. You're sick and tired of being careful all the time. I know all about it."

She had decided she wanted to cover up the earlier portrait, to observe Courbet's wishes and hide the original image. They had the X rays, evidence enough of the earlier ghost.

"You can't have everything," she told him.

He lined up her brushes according to thickness, arranged a row of blues from the palest icy one to the last, nearly black. "Show me the chemicals. I'll do it." He began to go through palette knives looking for a scraper. She grabbed his knobby wrists and could feel his watch digging into her palm, but in breaking free of her he knocked into a wall of shelves and every color in the universe came crashing down. Glass jars shattered, tubes were stepped on and paint gushed out of them. Dry pigment dust filled the air, clouds of cerulean mixed with puffs of rose, pools of coral spread into rivulets of amber and green. The guards rushed in. Colored footsteps were spattered all over. Waves of paint lapped the edges of frames.

The guards drew their guns.

"An accident," Anne said. "That's all it is. Sorry."

He ran out of the studio in his colored clothes, his footsteps led to the elevator, making a squishing sound as he ran. The guards asked who he was.

"Forget it," Anne told them. "Let's just call the night cleaners."

ANNE LOOKED for him in the elevator, and in the crowds wandering through the building upstairs. The newly issued revised list of staff telephone numbers was useless. She began to suspect the intruder was an impostor who didn't work in the museum at all. The painting was returned to Berlin, just as it was, all four eyes included. Tracy, one of the women who worked in the stockroom, said a friend of hers, a man who didn't have a job but liked to pass time in the museum, had disappeared recently, but she wouldn't admit whether or not he was the same person.

"Disappeared, I mean, I haven't heard from him in a while." She stopped herself from saying anything more about him. "Unauthorized people come and go all the time. If he, my friend, ran off to Berlin, I would have heard about it." She didn't know why he liked to spend so much time in the building. He owed her some money, but not much, so she equivocated, he might have just left without saying anything about it.

Tracy's hair was streaked Titian and firehouse red. She twisted a strand around a finger as she spoke and reminded Anne about the night the guards had to watch two naked white couples emerge from the Temple of Dendur. Society people had rented the Egyptian wing for a party, and the guards were told to pretend they weren't seeing anything. The next day one of them found a diamond bracelet that had been accidentally dropped in the Temple's narrow passageway.

"You know there isn't much space in there either. I mean what can two people do in the Temple of Dendur?"

"But I'm talking about the basement. Who would want to spend time here?"

"Once in a while runaways hide in the museum overnight. It's more congenial than Port Authority."

"Was your friend the kind of person who liked to pretend he was someone else? Did he shoplift his clothes?"

Tracy, herself a thief, looked at Anne as if she wanted to bolt. She was a little afraid of Anne because she worked in a different department and had what Tracy thought of as a real job. They were standing outside Anne's studio. The smell of solvent mixed with the perfume of curatorial assistants. Anne tried asking a few additional passersby, but none of the other basement workers really knew him, although they remembered him rushing around the corridors as if he had something to do. One man laughed at her and suggested she was seeing double.

Anne locked herself in her studio. The crackpot, whoever he was, would soon be forgotten. What did he have to do with deeply tanned men living in cities whose fortifications were originally built to keep out Ottoman Turks (while Turks living between city walls now endured harassment from within)? On television women who had multiple cosmetic surgeries talked about their transformative operations undertaken in order to look like Barbie, like the Mona Lisa, like Sharon Stone. The audience was perplexed. *I've seen a lot but you take the cake. Who do you think you are now?* Beside the screen lay an Anselm Keiffer book, but Anne didn't know what to do with the object. Its tarry and gritty pages were disintegrating. Flakes of one identity gave way to another, whether an interloper or a psychopath with a blow-torch were the agency of torment and disclosure. As the tele-vision droned on she wondered if one day someone would come along and reveal that underneath her concern for ad-versarial needs—exposure and preservation—lay . . . what? inertia, indifference, a chump easily conned? She picked up a rag and started cleaning the book. Hoping only paper and thread lay underneath its laden surface, and its secrets, its references, and its cartography could be kept private, she picked at an edge.

Asylum

SHE RODE UP the elevator with Krelnikov. They had both gotten to work early. Krelnikov made Eve nervous, but in her desire not to appear to be the kind of person who recoiled at any suggestion of confidentiality, she tried to hide her aversion to him and to act as if his insinuations were nothing serious.

"Hot day, again," he said.

The elevator was empty, but he stood close to her as if it were crowded, and he had intimate things to say.

"Nobody understands translation isn't an act of convenience. Every company wants their job toot sweet." He looked at her pleadingly. She wasn't in the mood for Krelnikov, didn't want to talk to him or figure out what he was trying to say.

"What do you want from me? What can I do about deadlines?"

"I'm sorry, Eve." He looked hurt.

She wondered what she had done and thought she would never stop apologizing to him.

Leaning against the polished steel paneling, he looked as if he'd spent days sitting on the edge of a chair in a dark room and could no longer stand up straight. Face wet from the heat, he punched a hole in the lid of his coffee cup and took a sip. Although he'd lived in New York for many years, he retained a strong accent.

"They forgot the sugar. You want this?"

"No thanks. I have my own. What are you working on?"

"I'm watching Spanish conquistadors travel up the Amazon. Their boats are beginning to take on water, and they swim with alligators. They haven't figured out how to make wallets."

"Are they lost in time?" Eve watched the lit numbers as the elevator slowly ascended, feeling Krelnikov's breath less than a foot away. She made up a story. "As the ship navigates a bend in the river they suddenly find a modern city with skyscrapers and an underground train system; they see men in suits, women in short skirts."

"No, it isn't that picture."

"How much time do you have left?"

"About ninety more minutes of the sixteenth century remains. Let me tell you I wouldn't mind a little civilization at this point: a village, a trading post, signs of a market economy. A group of Jesuits, I wouldn't mind," Krelnikov explained.

"It's in German?"

"Yes, of course, it's a German movie."

They reached the eleventh floor and the offices of Talk Around the Clock, Incorporated, a business that provided translation services for foreign-language films needing to be subtitled in English and American films requiring translation into other languages. The reception area was covered by movie posters unchanged for years: Jean Seberg, Judy Holliday, Orson Welles. Krelnikov stopped in front of Piper Laurie in *The Hustler* and imitated a pool shot, bending over so Eve had to walk around his butt. She guessed the coffee cup was supposed to be the ball at the point of his imaginary cue. Krelnikov and Eve went their separate ways. His office was to her left. The only kinds of movies he got excited about had to do with angels returning to earth as temporary humans or epics about great individuals. If he wanted to live his life over, if he wanted a second chance, Eve wondered what he was so desperate to erase, to tape over.

"Who wouldn't," he said, "grab at the opportunity to do something else in a younger body? You like romances and screwball comedies, which always seem opaque to me. I never laugh at mistaken identity, misplaced trust, or puns that I waste time trying to translate. You can keep your bedroom scenes and banana peels. Give me a second chance any day, and I'll grab it."

EVE WROTE in French as dialogue was spoken, then checked what she wrote against the film, and last of all, translated the dialogue or voice-over narration into English. She kept two sets of papers for each movie, the original and her translation. The mechanics of attaching subtitles to film was done at a lab. She threaded the film through the gates, one reel for sound, one reel for image. Usually she worked from an optical print, one reel alone. The room contained a Steenbeck editing table, a telephone, an extra chair, a shelf of English and foreign dictionaries. The blinds were drawn in order for Eve to see her work. A messenger brought cans of films from producers, and Dell, the receptionist, distributed the reels to Eve and the others.

Une femme inconnue

An unknown woman, Eve wrote quickly, *checked into a hotel.* The hotel looked like the kind of place where John Barrymore had contemplated suicide in *Dinner at Eight.* It was late afternoon, but the woman, whose short brown hair and black glasses were deceptive in their severity, fell asleep. When she awoke, it was the middle of the night. Her room was not shabby but not very well kept either. Its wallpaper appeared soft and worn. The bed, night table, and chairs looked as if they had been used and cleaned too many times. The camera pulled back to reveal a view across an airshaft, glowing dark blue and gray except for two squares of yellow light: windows. The hotel was designed so that it wrapped around a central courtyard. From an exterior shot

Eve quickly identified the unnamed city as New York. The telephone rang, and in a sleepy voice the actress answered it.

Yes, this is Corinne.

That established her name. Corinne hung up and returned to the window without switching on her lamp. Beside a long striped curtain she stood very still. There was music on the sound track, uninterrupted by dialogue or voice-over. Eve fast-forwarded. Suddenly Corinne saw a man and woman struggling. Their fight seemed partly a drunken brawl, but then the woman, a blonde whose hair was twisted up in the back of her head, gave a final push. The man went over the edge and down the airshaft. The blonde woman didn't scream or appear distraught. She wiped her hands on her skirt as if she'd just dirtied them and fingered the stray wisps that had escaped her twist in the effort. Less than a minute passed, but in movie time, it wasn't clear how long she sat in the room where the man had been murdered. Eve noticed the sky on the little screen of the Steenbeck editing table growing lighter. The police came. The woman was, or pretended to be, grief-stricken, as if the fall had been an accident. She handed them a letter, which they read, nodding, handling it with gloves and tweezers, then putting the paper in a plastic bag. The police went away. The woman ran a comb over her tightly twisted hair without undoing it, picked up her keys, and prepared to go out. Corinne cleaned her glasses on a shirttail, put on her jacket, intending to trail her. The camera followed the two women as one and then the other passed an appliance store whose signs were in Arabic. Washing machines, hair driers, cameras, and radios all glowed in the shadows behind the grating. Corinne dogged the other woman's steps as she went into a drugstore, and pretended to look at magazines and birthday cards while the blonde woman waited for a prescription to be filled, struggling but failing to overhear what was said.

Dell knocked on her door. Before answering, Eve froze

the two women who, once back at the hotel, had walked the corridors circling the airshaft only to bump into one another at the elevator. They came face to face but still behaved like the strangers they were.

"I'm going home, Eve. You'll be the last one in the studio tonight."

"When did Krelnikov leave?"

"A half hour ago, but he might be coming back. Sometimes he leaves early on Friday, sometimes not."

"Have a good weekend."

"I wouldn't hang around here alone, you know. People get ideas and what not. You should go home."

So far there hadn't been much dialogue; the job was mainly voice-over. She rubbed her eyes and told Dell to wait for her, writing: *The woman who just gave you her key, what was her name?* before turning off the machine. Eve marked her place, rewound the film and left the office.

Complaining of the heat, Dell stopped to buy a Mister Softee from a truck parked at a corner. The tinkling music blaring from a speaker in the front seat of the Mister Softee van gave Eve a headache, but at the same time she found it oddly soothing and out of place on an urban street where the song had as much impact as a car horn that played the theme from *The Godfather* over and over again. As they walked to the subway Eve imagined Krelnikov wandering aimlessly around the city before returning to a long night of work, staring at shop displays, looking over the shoulder of someone busy with Space Wizard or Donkey Kong.

"PEOPLE WILL do anything to get an apartment," Mr. O'Neill said. He often sat out on the steps in front of their building reading newspapers or thrillers he found in the trash or on the street. He claimed to be the lost son of Eugene O'Neill.

"What do you mean?"

"Two men, both from Iron Curtain countries," he explained, "shared a place over on East Seventh Street, but the name of only one of them appeared on the lease. The other, you see, had just arrived, and had been here no more than a few weeks. He murdered the first guy, cut up his body, took the dead man's credit card, went to the hardware store and bought trash bags to dispose of the parts. He might have gotten away with it, too, if it hadn't been a long weekend, but it was the Fourth of July and hot, you know, so naturally the corpse in the dumpster began to smell. When the man was caught, he claimed that his only motive had been to get his name on the lease. He just wanted his own apartment. I haven't seen your friend Lenny around lately. Does he have another job that took him to California again?"

"He just wanted an apartment of his own," Eve said.

When she got upstairs she looked up the name of Corinne's hotel in the telephone book. She thought she might walk by it sometime, just because she enjoyed seeing places she knew in the movies and seeing places where films had been shot. Hotel des Fauves, Hotel Curry, Hotel Development Assocs, Hotel Dexter, Hotel Dixie, Hotel Fane Dumas, Hotel Franconia. It wasn't listed.

THE MURDERESS didn't guess she was being followed. Corinne managed to break into her hotel room and read some letters. While she was going through the papers, the camera cut to the other woman entering the hotel, stopping for her messages at the front desk. Eve didn't like suspense. It made her feel helpless. She resisted speeding ahead to get the tension over with. There was a lot of cutting back and forth between the two women, each getting closer to the point where they would meet. Eve had to translate the contents of one letter as it was held up to the camera. She wasn't sure how much of it was important, but since only a small part of the text would fit in the margin left for subtitles she had to make a decision.

Eve underlined *Dear Martine, Meet me at 2:00 at the train station under the clock.* That seemed the essential message but she wasn't certain. The blonde woman now had a name, Martine, and Martine was on her way back to her room. While she stopped down the hall to speak to one of the maids, Corinne slipped out of her room, running quickly around the corner, and so her surveillance continued undetected.

At two o'clock the following afternoon Corinne saw Martine meet a man under a clock at a train station. There was a long embrace and a long kiss but no dialogue and no voice-over. Eve fast-forwarded. She didn't want to watch. Then the man was taken up to her hotel room.

As Corinne became increasingly obsessed with watching Martine, she began to neglect the reasons for her own trip to the unnamed city. She was a buyer for a French department store and had come to the city to place orders for American T-shirts and sunglasses. Angry telephone messages and notes revealed that while caught up in her fixation with Martine she failed to return calls or attend meetings. Samples of merchandise were sent to her room in vain. Boxes and bags piled near the door. She became convinced that Martine would murder again, and in order to stop her, if that's what Corinne really wanted to do, she had to determine Martine's motives.

What linked the two men, one dead, one not yet so, together? Eve wrote, translating Corinne's voice-over thoughts as she looked out the window, watching, waiting to see if they, too, would fight. *One-notyetso,* Eve said out loud. The phrase sounded like a kind of martial arts gesture, but she left it.

"Give up, Corinne," Eve shouted into the air, "Martine and her friend are getting along like a house on fire." Krelnikov banged on the wall.

Corinne finally opened the boxes, scattering lids across

the floor. She tried on all the sunglasses and T-shirts, then took them off. Outside all was black until Martine suddenly turned on a light, appearing naked as she walked around the hotel suite. The man she had met in the train station got out of bed, too. They began to dress, but soon abandoned the task, and the two of them could be seen lying on the floor. Corinne stood behind the curtain again, hand over her mouth, laughing, *Ah mon dieu.*

EVE RAN into Dell in the bathroom, a series of lefts down a half-green, half-gray hall. She leaned into the mirror holding her eyes open, putting on mascara.

"That Mr. K, he takes too many breaks and comes out of his room to disturb me when I have my own work to do. I'm sick of listening to his crabbing. He makes me feel like I work on the complaint hot line at the Department of Transportation. All I can do is listen and say 'Please hold,' then he yells at me as if he thinks I should be taking notes. I tell you this, if I worked for the city I'd probably get paid more than I ever got out of Talk Around the Clock." Dell jabbed the air with her mascara wand.

"Are you staying late tonight?"

"No. No chance."

"I'll probably work all night."

"No job's worth it, if you ask me."

"I'm behind deadline."

Eve had tried to get the company to pay for cabs when she had to work late nights but the accountant, a retired chiseler named Dumphreys who worked part-time, would look at her over the top of his bifocals and tell her they were low on petty cash.

"All right, I'm leaving, you talked me into it again. If anyone asks why this job isn't finished tell them I had to leave early because I was sick. Back me up."

"Krelnikov will rat."

They walked back to the reception area. Dell dumped ashes from the New York Sheraton ashtray she kept on her desk into an overflowing trash can.

"I've been working enough overtime to make up for it."

They were still talking when the elevator doors opened. Krelnikov jumped when he saw them. He was eating a doughnut, and his mouth was ringed with powdered sugar. He wiped his hands on his pants, saying, "Eleventh floor already. Going out for some air?"

"Yes," she lied to him.

"It's hot in my office, too."

"The air conditioner is on, Mr. K," Dell said.

"There isn't enough separation between church and state in this business, Dell." He said this as if he knew something, had seen things they couldn't begin to imagine. He often spoke this way, talking down to them in deeply inflected syllables.

Dell shrugged. Eve interpreted his statement to mean that he was still working on the jungle film and felt everywhere he went was suffocating, humid, and each transaction he faced, from ordering lunch to buying a lottery ticket, was as hopeless as conquistadors swimming with alligators.

**PROSTITUTE SLAYING LINKED TO SECRETARY OF STATE
DRUG CZAR SNAGS DOMESTIC KINGPIN
MY DAUGHTER WILL KNOW THE TRUTH**

Mr. O'Neill was throwing out old papers. As her eye traveled across the stacks the headlines became increasingly alarmist. He had combed his hair back from his head and was wearing an ancient but elegant suit. By taking out the garbage in a jacket with satin lapels Eve felt O'Neill was unveiling his pretensions to celebrity for all to see, but the exposure revealed only how vulnerable his aspirations were, how open he was to ridicule and curbside dirt. She hung around to talk to him, afraid he would be shoved aside by a crowd of children or an indiscriminate garbage man.

"Car got broken into down the street," he said.

"Happens all the time, Mr. O'Neill."

"This one was full of heads."

"Heads? Not real heads?"

"No, they weren't real. They were models for Downstate Medical Center's ocular unit, but the guys who broke into the car didn't know that. They sure didn't."

"What did they do?"

"They screamed. What would you do?"

"I wouldn't break into a car."

"No, you wouldn't."

Eve wasn't sure this was meant as encouragement. O'Neill sat on a stack of papers and crossed his legs.

"Ever translate *Anna Christie?*"

"No, I don't do old movies. If it was ever translated the job was done years ago."

"I met Garbo when she was working on the movie. My father took me to meet her. She held my face in her hands. 'Such a beautiful boy,' she said, 'I will never forget you.' I thought that since she lived in New York, she might want to visit me these last years. She never answered my letters."

"I think she was a recluse."

"Who in their right mind wouldn't be?"

"Well, nuts to her."

"That's what I say. Eve, will you do me a favor?"

Eve knew this meant a trip to Liquor Plus down the street.

"I used to look at people in the city as a series of open books, or open to different degrees. Now people are video games." He made binging and bonging noises as he adjusted the papers. Then he straightened up and pretended he was ramming and turning knobs, speeding around a computerized road, ramming other cars, zapping running figures whose knees lifted at ninety-degree angles. If you didn't know what he thought he was doing, he looked obscene.

When Eve turned to make her way toward Liquor Plus someone turned on a fire hydrant, but no children or dogs ran through the water, and it poured into the gutter, rushing toward the stacks of papers O'Neill had so carefully assembled.

"Your friend," someone said, "is going to get wet, and so are you." Eve turned around quickly. A group of men standing in front of a laundromat didn't seem aware that she existed. One of them was sucking a Sugar Daddy, and he threw the yellow and red wrapper into the stream of water. A few of them laughed, but she couldn't tell if they were laughing at her. She couldn't tell which one, if any, had threatened.

SHE FELL asleep in the editing room. The others had long gone. Eve lay on the floor telling herself she would rest for only a few minutes, but when she awoke, it was hours later. The room was nearly pitch-black; the only light came from the square image on the editing table. Tiny Corinne had stood watching tiny Martine for hours. The square had a ghostly green light. The room smelled of sticky celluloid. Eve wanted to go home, but home seemed too far and too complicated a trip, even though it was only one fairly short subway ride. She lay down on the floor again, staring at the ceiling this time without sleeping. She thought she heard sounds from Krelnikov's room next door, a sound like a drawer opening, but she couldn't be sure. Perhaps the translator who liked angels and epics did live in his office.

Corinne asked for her messages at the hotel desk, but seeing Martine enter the hotel, she dawdled at the counter, pretending to read American Express brochures, while Martine asked for her messages. She was told that a Charles Vague called. *Vag, pas Vaig,* Martine corrected the clerk's pronunciation. Eve didn't know what to do with this line. In voice-over, because the whole incident was being remem-

bered, Corinne wondered if he might be some kind of partner of Martine's, rather than a potential victim.

"Finally, you figure something out," Eve said.

Corinne looked up Vague in the telephone book. The
camera followed her short red nail down a column of print.
There was only one Vague listed. After a telephone call,
Corinne determined that he was a taxidermist and his
company was located downtown, so far west the city was
no longer recognizable as itself. There were empty windy
avenues with wide garages and loading docks for trucks.
Corinne, on the pretense of wanting a parrot stuffed, went
to pay a visit to Monsieur Vague, but as she got out of the
cab, she saw Martine enter the Vague door, staggering under
the weight of an enormous package. Corinne stood in a doorway, watching her from the street. She waited by an empty
loading dock, watching as minutes passed. (An hour, Eve
figured, in real time.) Finally Martine emerged again,
empty-handed, and got into a waiting car.

Watching Corinne climb the dark stairs to Charles
Vague's studio Eve felt the walls moving in. As she rang the
taxidermist's bell, Eve imagined a disaster in which Talk
Around the Clock would be blown up, film frames flying in
all directions. Little bits of burnt celluloid like black plastic
snow would fall on the sidewalk, on a fire truck, into a stack
of newspapers at the corner stand.

Corinne knocked on the pebbled glass door at the top of
the landing, then opened it. The room was filled, not only
with stuffed animals but old glass cabinets, dusty over-
stuffed chairs, and stacks of unshelved books. Monsieur
Vague introduced himself and asked what he could do for
her. Looking concerned, Corinne told him she possessed a
dying parrot that meant the world to her and when it passed
away, she would like to have it stuffed. Vague was younger
and more fashionable than Eve imagined a taxidermist
would look.

How long have you had this parrot?
Five years.
What is it dying of?
The cause of illness has the veterinarian puzzled.
"She's an excellent liar," Eve said.

"I don't want to hear about it, please!" Krelnikov banged on the wall. He was in.

Eve turned down the sound. Vague asked for Corinne's number, saying he would send someone round to collect the parrot. She gave it to him, but insisted the bird wasn't dead yet, and there was a chance, however slight, that it might recover. *So please don't call me. I'll call you.* Eve thought, you dope, you should never have given him the number at the hotel. You'll die now.

Unable to wait herself, she fast-forwarded. Corinne, showing equal parts stupidity and courage, broke into the taxidermist's to search the place at night. The plot was simple. Martine and Vague were smuggling all kinds of things out in the animals. Drugs, computer viruses, diamonds, all sealed in Florida alligators, bald eagles, and mountain lions. In close-ups, paws were carefully slit or feathers spilled in the search. It was a diverse business, specializing in endangered species. The men Martine murdered in various ways had each been investigating her connection to Vague. She let them trace her to her hotel room, and she let them think they were acting as seducers. She was very good at what she did, and Corinne admired her as her own life as a buyer for Printemps had been without adventure or romance. This was indicated by the irate callers and other signs of her dull, quotidian responsibilities. The sunglasses and T-shirts lying in piles were indistinguishable from one another. The film didn't go into it, but Eve imagined Corinne must have lost her job after spending weeks evading salesmen and obsessively following the woman across the airshaft. Apart from the accident at the elevator, the two never met.

Just before the very end, Eve went backwards. She was shocked by what she saw. Vague was in Corinne's hotel room. He drew the striped curtains. The room grew very dark. He threatened Corinne, but it wasn't clear to Eve, who had been skipping around, how much either one of them knew about the other. Corinne took off her clothes slowly, and then Vague, too, undressed.

"He looks like a shirt ad," Eve whispered. "He's too perfect and too sinister. I don't believe she would let herself be seduced. The man probably smells of preserving chemicals. Some people will do anything to get what?"

"Pleasure in danger," Krelnikov said. "Don't you understand?" He had opened her door, just as Vague approached Corinne.

"Hi. My name's Vague. Charles Vague." He imitated James Bond with an exaggerated accent. Either he had been standing there for a while or could hear more through the walls than Eve had imagined possible.

"You had me fooled, Mr. K. Look, I have to finish this translation by tomorrow." She didn't say leave me alone.

"Just let me distract you for a moment. I'm done with the film about the Amazon." He turned off Eve's editing table, and the room instantly became dark. "I'm working on something else I want to show you."

Eve didn't want to be rude to him, she was always rude to him, but she was afraid of Krelnikov's tiny editing room where his size and neediness filled the office. The last time he had called her in, he had been translating a scene from a science fiction film in which digital waiters served dinners to humans, pouring wine and slicing rare meat with the grace of pre-Industrial Revolution etiquette in spite of their microchip hearts. It had been a story of revenge, predictable but disturbing. Sandblasted by Krelnikov's moroseness and misanthropy she marked her place, then turned her notes over. He noticed her gesture.

"I don't want to read your translation. I don't care who the murderer is. I mean, I already know."

"I can only look for a minute, then I have to get back."

A MAN picked up half a brick from the rubble on the street and broke the glass window of a building that appeared abandoned. Its doors were boarded up; some of the windows had bars over them, but the bars were twisted in different directions as if a strong wind blowing close to the ground had swept through. Layers of dirt accumulated so densely over the decoration of the lower storeys that what had once been ornate were now like a series of blackened chunks. No longer specific; cornices, keystones, or gargoyles melted into clusters of lumps.

"It was called the Canary Island Rest Stop Hotel," said Krelnikov. "This is a part of the city in which many buildings have been abandoned. Nobody has figured how they can make any money through reclamation, so the empty offices and lofts stay empty, you see. Subways stop at the edge of the district bringing in Vietnamese and Turks who work in airless sweatshops."

"This is a German movie?"

"Yes, of course. Why do you always ask me that? It's supposed to be Berlin. You can see trucks filled with bolts of cloth, and racks of dresses and suits clog the alleys by day. At night everything, even the diners, is closed."

"Diners? You've been here too long."

"Cafés. I wanted you to understand."

"The loading bays look as if they were shot a few blocks away."

"No, I don't think so." Krelnikov was breathing hard.

The Canary Island Rest Stop still had erratically supplied electricity. Squatters lived somewhere in its recesses. There were points of light which gleamed from upper balconies looking out onto the lobby. A bank of lit elevators in a glass shaft, lambent and mesmerizing, seemed to travel without stopping.

"What goes on in the upper floors?"

"I don't know. The stairwells are completely black."

The man began to climb one spiraling flight, a series of matches illuminating his face as he ascended. His head was shaved, covered by tattoos. Gradually the sound of other voices appeared on the sound track. The man followed the murmur of the voices until he came to a room on what Eve figured must have been the fourth floor. Down a dark hall, a few light bulbs sputtered overhead, but finally he pushed open a door to find a Vietnamese family squatting on the floor, eating a communal meal. Light hit their white bowls; they looked up at the intruder, alarmed.

"You're going to have to find someone to translate the Vietnamese," Eve said.

"No, they only want the German translated." The man pulled out a knife, and Krelnikov abruptly turned off the machine.

"He's going to kill them."

"How do you know? Where's the angel?"

"Whoever said there would be one? There aren't any. So what I want you to do is listen to this scene while I'm in the hall, then tell me if any German is spoken in it."

"I don't do German. Only French." She immediately regretted her answer.

"But you know what it sounds like. I can't watch this scene, and I may not have to if there's no speech in it."

"It's late, Krelnikov. I have to go home."

INSANE LIQUIDATORS   INSANE LIQUIDATORS   INSANE LIQUIDATORS

Eve ran past cut-rate stores that sold piles of merchandise: blenders, toasters, computers. Past window displays of gold chains arranged like starfish and past men who asked what her name was. That night the city was a kind of schizophrenic whose personalities had aged differently. Some parts of the landscape had been rejuvenated from an injection of redevelopment, new if ugly. Others fell to pieces. Window gates peeled away, pried off their hinges like a lattice made of dough. The fire escapes were crowded. A city full of people who may believe they're being gypped out of their true identity and recognition; a city full of people like Krelnikov who wanted to live their lives all over again. What secrets would she bury in stuffed trophies, hunted and endangered, then mail out of the country? She couldn't think of any. She envied Dell, who did her eyes three times a day and couldn't care less.

On her way home Eve looked through the flyblown labels in Liquor Plus and the chicken dinners for two (fries and cornbread included), all for $7.95, which were sold next door. She couldn't imagine the city where fashionable women gave up on T-shirts and sunglasses, and followed a murderer because perhaps they wanted to kill someone too, but hadn't ever the nerve, and so tailed a woman who did. Even as she had waited for the elevator she could hear the sound of the translator in the room next to her, sobbing and rewinding film. You couldn't, she learned, tell him it was just a story, because he had been in that city, and he knew it was all true.

Fishwanda

1

PLAYING ON the third floor of Loew's Thirty-fourth Street Multiplex, in Cineplex 3: *Fishwanda.* The abbreviation as it traveled around the dot board sounded as if someone were reading a map accordion-folded between Africa and India. I went on to the next level to see *Midnight Run.* Robert De Niro chased a Mafia accountant from Brooklyn to Las Vegas, and afterwards as we walked down Second Avenue we repeated lines from the movie. *Do I know you? Wait a minute, I don't think I know you.* We instinctively understood that De Niro was referring to *Taxi Driver* even in this much later movie and it's funny. We know the language. We get the joke. *Fishwanda,* seen briefly in a preview, disappeared, forgotten. On lower Second Avenue we passed the Telephone Bar and Grill whose front was constructed from a series of English telephone boxes. They could be copies, but they look real enough. One red box is actually the entrance to the bar. I continue to be surprised all those little panes of glass haven't been smashed in, but a metal door comes down at night and the neighborhood is full of tourists anyway.

2

MONEY WAS supposed to be wired to her soon from somewhere. As she walked from the post office empty-handed, she pretended to be an American tourist, one who could leave in a few days, one for whom the trip would soon be nothing more than a few travel stories and postcards. She wasn't sure she wanted to return, but seemed not to have much choice anymore, and so she stayed.

She stood before Constables and Turners and imagined that the smugglers, escaped convicts, and drenched fishermen who stood by watching a boat break on a choppy sea were replaced by Iroquois. Small towns far to the north of England that had no electricity or telegraphs, whose citizens banked on lake monsters, these hamlets might not be so different from northern towns near the Canadian border. The English versions might not know or care that Wall Street had crashed. What does it mean that a market has "crashed"? Boom, a couple of awnings tumble, a horse runs away, apples roll into the gutter. Remote American towns might by now have read about Black October and stockbrokers jumping from windows, fortunes utterly lost, but the crash mightn't mean all that much to them either, in those places with names like Chateaugay, Champlain, Swanton, and Saddleback. She hadn't yet determined what it was going to mean to her. Maybe nothing, but as she waited for money that didn't seem to be coming, it was fairly certain the crash was going to mean something. American travelers became stranded in Europe and turned into expatriates or exiles, shadowy amalgamations of foreign manners with shreds of familiar accents, but it didn't seem possible that this hybridization would happen to her, not in 1928, even with a crash. The money to return home would have to come. Mercurial changes in painted light were due to fog, not smoke signals. She tried to remember the Hudson River as she had traveled down it by train and the weather seemed constant although she knew it wasn't. In memory, when the sun shone over Rhinebeck, it would be bright in Rhinecliff as well and all the way down to New York. In London she lost umbrella after umbrella, as if with each accidental leaving behind lay the idea that she might not need that particular umbrella again. She left the museum and walked to her rooms to save money.

When she had arrived from France she was supposed to contact friends of her father but the bag that had contained their addresses had been lost or stolen (she wasn't sure how it had disappeared), and with its absence the connections which were supposed to help her navigate England were severed. Weeks passed, but she didn't bother to try to look up the names she did remember. After traveling around the continent to a constellation of cities linked by who her father knew, it was a relief to cross the Channel alone and to arrive at a place where it was not such a struggle to make herself understood. While taking walks alone, she pretended the streets and parks she traversed were familiar. She invented an artificial history for herself, one of privilege, in part like her American past, but with distant relatives living in colonies who would send her ivory totems from Nairobi, tea from Ceylon, a three-eyed, many-armed brass devi with a moon on her head. The reality of a painted postcard of a log cabin and box of arrowheads disappeared. As long as her money held out, and she didn't open her mouth, she could almost make the phony history stick.

She rented rooms from a woman whose husband had died in Suez and left her a small income and a house in Whitcher Place. The widow claimed to be particular about who she let to and told her a great deal about the other lodgers: a musician and a German student, both women, and one man who claimed to be some kind of linguist. His room was closest to hers, and she often saw him coming and going. They were introduced in the hall, and while brushing something that looked like ash from his cuffs he told her he was working on a glossary of regional expressions and slang terminology. His declaration came out of nowhere and was spoken assertively as if his right to stand in the hall might have been questioned if he hadn't stated his purported occupation. She could almost see corridor objects, a lamp, a potted plant, reflected in his slicked-back hair and wondered what he put in it to make his hair so gluey-looking and all of a piece. At night, through the thin wall between her room and his, he could be heard repeating phrases to himself.

The landlady was afraid of the linguist, but pestered him about rent nonetheless, and snooped in his room when he was out. She knew he was the kind of person who drove women round the twist, she said that he was born to chase a bob without success, and that he left queer books lying around. The young American visitor didn't know what she was talking about, but the landlady was a chatterbox, especially when she needed reinforcement or a boost of morale after a run-in with the sponge.

"I even lent him money when he first arrived, and I've been very lenient with this man, but generosity on my part isn't without limits, *my girl.*"

She pretended to agree with her, suspecting that her time for trying the landlady's leniency would be next.

Weak threats did nothing to terminate the whispering on the other side of the wall about the five different meanings of *how's your father* and the etymology of *knackered, Bob's your uncle,* and *taking the piss out of* . . . what? With her ear to the wall she couldn't quite hear the end of his sentence though she held her breath and strained to catch what he spoke into the damp air of early evening.

One afternoon when the prying landlady was out at the shops, he asked her if she would meet him at the British Museum, but only if she were going near the West End that day. He insisted it wasn't important, jingling the keys in his pocket to emphasize his nonchalance, but she grew flustered under what she perceived as his scrutiny. For days she had talked to no one, counted her remaining pounds, and waited for the fare to return home.

"I'll meet you in the Egyptian wing, near a fragment of papyrus that is labeled 'The Opening of the Mouth Ceremony.'"

Well, all right. She didn't know what to think of his solicitation but kept the appointment because she had nothing else to do, and so standing around the Egyptian wing she waited for him, reading all the labels as she did so. *This ritual restored to the mummy all his faculties so that he might enjoy the afterlife to the full.* He was twenty minutes late, as if the minutes had been timed exactly, as if he knew the limits of her patience and capacity for boredom. He took her arm, and she felt repulsion at his solicitous touch, but didn't remove it.

He took her to a pub near the center of London where it was unlikely they would be noticed. From where she sat she could see him at the bar accepting their drinks from the barman, then looking in his wallet, putting a few coins on the bar and shaking his head. He said something to the man, then returned to their table asking if he could borrow some money. He was short. She knew he had come to the conclusion, perhaps fueled by the landlady's imagination, that she was a rich American traveling alone without friends or family and therefore an easy mark. Nonetheless she gave him what he claimed was the difference, watching him pocket the change the barman gave him.

"Tell me about the Dutch houses with ziggurat rooftops and red Indians," he would ask, pretending he was interested. "Describe the historic fort, the table with a colonist's dried blood on it that's never been cleaned. Whose blood do you think it is really? Maybe it's a recent murder after all." He said foolish things, but she kept on spending time with him.

After a few conversations she realized he didn't actually listen to her; he often asked her the same questions. It was as if he were memorizing her life so he could sail to New York, adopt a different accent, and claim to be a long lost relative due a piece of her fortune that hadn't been considerable and might all be gone now.

When she watched boxes of books removed from his rooms as he was gradually forced to sell off his library she felt sorry for him. Bit by bit she found herself giving him money she didn't have. After drinks, although she continued to find him repellent, she kept waiting for him to do more than take her arm, feeling like she was acting on a dare, taking risks over something she didn't really want anyway. He hesitated, as if he were waiting for her, and then he would launch into translations of East End rhyming slang.

At breakfast one morning he grew nervous, then left in a hurry. She was disappointed that he hadn't arranged to meet her during the afternoon or even later on. Hurrying from the table she caught him in the hall as he put on his hat. *Later, my dear,* he said, and he kissed her quickly when the landlady's back was turned. Upstairs, alone, feeling left out of something she couldn't define, she looked through a pile of books left by his door. She picked up *London Labour and the London Poor,* Henry Mayhew, and began to read a passage that had been marked.

> "I continued walking the streets for three years, sometimes making a good deal of money, sometimes none, feasting one day and starving the next. The bigger girls could persuade me to do anything they liked with my money. I was never happy all the time, but I could get no character and could not get out of the life. I lodged all this time at a lodging-house in Kent Street. They were all thieves and bad girls. I have known between three and four dozen boys and girls sleep in one room. The beds were horrid filthy and full of vermin. There was very wicked carryings on. I can't go into the particulars but whatever could take place between boys and girls squeedged into one bed, did take place and in the midst of the others."

She shut the book and walked out, down Camden High Street, Hampstead Road, past clumps of schoolchildren in uniforms, prams, and grocers with horse-drawn carts. She walked and walked, up Shaftesbury Avenue, Holborn Viaduct, she gave nothing to buskers, veterans of the Great War, gassed blind, missing limbs, clinking cups, Cheapside, Threadneedle, Bishopsgate to Spitalfields. She circled back, stopping at Cleopatra's Needle, leaning over, looking at the river. It was growing dark, and she saw women walking through the park alone or in pairs, speaking to men who came along their way. At first she thought they were asking the time or inquiring after directions, then she realized they were soliciting passersby. Each transaction was watched by a man who stood some distance away, unnoticed but vigilant. She thought she saw her neighbor from Whitcher Place but couldn't be sure it was he, and not wanting to run into him, she took a different path out of the park. What had he been up to? What if she did the same thing, whatever that thing might be? A night spent on a bench or under a tree in a remote part of Regent's Park would be haunted by those who earned their keep within its boundaries, and then returning in a disheveled state, her landlady might assume the worst and not let her in again. She could make up a story, say she suffered temporary amnesia, or that she was knocked unconscious by thieves and all her money was gone, but she doubted she could make such a story come across in a believable way. By the time she returned to Whitcher Place night had fallen.

On the first floor, a radio had been left on. *Trio Snotta in F,* an announcer's voice said. The room was empty. She reached into a cabinet and turned the radio off. The pretense fell apart. As long as she had money, she could pretend she had always been here, but the prospect of destitution tested her false history in a way which made her feel it wasn't her fault. She didn't know the language.

On the second stairwell she could see the landlady peering from the doorway of the linguist's room, pink with anger. *Look,* she said, *he's left, bolted, owing three months' back rent.* She looked in. The room was nearly bare. His books and clothes, all his things were gone; he had even stolen bits of worthless china and a lamp. He had given his name as E. Thomas Reardon, and it turned out to be a pseudonym, so checks left on the mantle were useless, and he must have known that they would be. She had gone right to the bank with them when she'd discovered he'd gone. *Why did he bother to write them out?* the landlady asked, hoodwinked and insulted.

She was hungry and sorry she'd turned off the radio. The landlady stared at her in an uncomfortable silence. She felt tired and cold from all her walking, her shoes badly worn, and without thinking she asked the landlady if he had left a note for her. Only afterward did she realize how foolish her request sounded. Foolish in that it gave a great deal away to the other woman, and she could tell the woman looked at her as someone who could be aggressive and perhaps a bit vulgar, someone who said things which ought never even to have been thought.

"Do you know what he did? Do you know what he really did?"

She remembered the underlined passage and the sighting in the park. A gentleman scholar down at the heels who wasn't what he claimed. What does working on a lexicon of slang signify anyway? Making accessible, breaking barriers which seal a locale or language group, trying to let one cluster of people into the secrets of another. She envisioned a little man in a plaid suit brandishing a crowbar which he would use toward this end, but the dictionary project was a meaningless front, a hoax. The landlady pointed again to the empty room. She didn't know what to say. The landlady looked at her with suspicion as she backed into her room, and in her hostile stare lay accusations of unimaginable dimensions. She resolved again that as long as she remained in London she wouldn't speak to anyone. She would be as if mute.

3

ELEANOR MARX left Liverpool for New York on August 31, 1886. She was thirty-one years old. The first Americans she observed were on the boat and she wrote, "They laughed at the poor immigrants lying on the deck in their wretched clothes . . . without the least sign of sympathy."

She was seen with a man in a loud checkered suit who favored bright ties. Edward Aveling's interests in the signs of class were not the same as Eleanor's. *Nobody is as bad as Aveling looks.* Her friends, with the exception of Engels, loathed him. He was the great love of her life. In photographs his face looks pasty and his expression petulant; it would contradict his reputation as a seducer, and of his alluring voice there is no record. Besides women he was pursued by financial scandals. All that remains of his seductiveness are the historical traces of infamy and disrepute, a man remembered for inventive schemes designed to benefit only himself.

In a letter posted shortly before departure, Aveling wrote, half ironically, but perhaps also partly believing the possibility existed, that he might make millions of dollars in America. He was to see the beginnings of the great urban slums of New York and Chicago, and he must have had some sense of this if they were going to speak to American working people, but still, there was the mythology, the possibility of millions of dollars waiting to be made. Though not an out-and-out cheapskate, he was thought the kind of man who would try to squeeze a shilling into a pound by whatever means. On board the ship he invariably tried to hoodwink other people, even a cabin boy, into paying for his sherry. He was to have one heroic moment in America although the mythological fortune eluded him.

He looked over the women in the ship's dining room, just checking, a few glanced his way. There were opportunities to flirt with other passengers, moments when young American women returning from a long European tour left mothers and aunts below deck and, standing a few feet away from Edward, stared out at the Atlantic. He could do little more than watch porpoises and gulls with them. He might have listened to them complain of how stifling an aunt could be when one wanted to wander around London alone, or how one got sick in Venice or Paris, but he could only touch an elbow in a caricature of sympathy or pat a sea-sprayed hand. Ten days on the ocean gave him a few chances to visit the cabins of single women, but until they arrived in New York, there were no places to escape once the liaison ended, however passionately, halfheartedly, or ephemerally it had begun. If he needed to give the object of his desire the slip, he would have to hide in steerage or the boiler room, an unpleasant prospect. (Even in the cause of evasion, Aveling was not known to have spoken to any workers during the course of his tour.) A boat was not the best place for the kind of romance Aveling preferred. As rumors circulated within its confines, Eleanor would surely discover his infidelities. He leaned over the rail and watched porpoises and gulls. Except for the burial at sea of a woman traveling to meet her husband, it was a dull voyage. Once in New York he couldn't disappear into the city either. If he could have, if he had no responsibilities, he would rent hotel rooms, write plays, and go to auditions. He would meet American women of all kinds whose faces he imagined would reflect mixed nationalities, and he would tell them he was an actor who had performed before the queen. The American women wouldn't have seen his picture. They wouldn't know that his trip had been sponsored by the Socialist Labor Party of North America and his time, if he stuck to his commitments, was to be all booked up.

The Statue of Liberty had just arrived from Paris and was being assembled so it was not in New York harbor when they arrived. Lower Manhattan must have looked confusing to them as several different neighborhoods met at the end of the island, at Coenties Slip. Already the New World was not easily reduced to one thing. These contradictory elements drew Eleanor's first image of New York: smokestacks, horse-drawn carts, the steeple of Trinity Church, ship chandlers' offices, and English spoken in unfamiliar accents. The black metallic S curve of the elevated train shadowed the squalor of the Lower East Side which had recently learned to grow under it.

They were taken deeper into that neighborhood, and Eleanor wrote to her sister Laura that she considered New York a "very dirty, shoddy town." She stayed in the apartment of Wilhelm Rosenberg at 261 East Tenth Street between First Avenue and Avenue A. It is a street of tenements and railroad apartments and Rosenberg's apartment was one of these. She didn't think to compare the German-speaking neighborhood to Spitalfields or the East End. It was dirty and shoddy in a way that was very symbolic of New York: square blocks, square buildings, several storeys higher than English ones, packed full of people, no yards, no gardens, not even paltry ones with soot-covered plants.

Eleanor and Aveling spoke to 25,000 people at Cooper Union, a school for artists, architects, and engineers. The building is large, brown, a series of Romanesque arches in tiers spanning Astor Place and Cooper Square. There is a small triangular park behind it, and the crowd may have spilled out from the Great Hall. That night there was one Buddeke present, a Pinkerton agent. The Pinkerton organization was founded by a Scotsman who immigrated to

Chicago. Originally the Pinkertons were detectives, but they became known for spying on union organizers and breaking strikes by violent means. Buddeke, probably a German immigrant, was actually hired to tail Wilhelm Liebknecht, but on their American tours Liebknecht's and Eleanor's paths intersected. (In a sense they must have worked in tandem since Liebknecht, whose English wasn't very good, addressed primarily German-speaking crowds. Eleanor and Aveling were able to reach non-German-speaking Americans.) When Eleanor spoke at Cooper Union police entered the crowd and tried to disrupt the meeting. As she saw movement near the doors Eleanor said, "I have been told that you in America enjoy such freedom that socialism is not needed. Well, all you seem to enjoy is being shot by Pinkertons. I speak not only of what I have seen, but of what I have read in your labor statistics. You have no more freedom than us." Buddeke wrote bits of her speech into a notebook as he examined those around him and made note of the enthusiastic individuals who happened to be standing nearby, describing dress, attitude, or making little sketches. At the same time he tried to determine the identities of the Americans on the podium. He was kept very busy.

When he saw the blue uniforms of the New York police, did Buddeke show them some sort of identification or did he just leave? To flash a badge was to risk someone in the crowd remembering his face and in the future, on another job, he could be fingered as the stoolie he truly was. His cover would have been blown. On the other hand, by refraining from identifying himself he risked being bludgeoned or arrested. Photographs of Eleanor Marx survive but Buddeke's image has vanished. His bill for spying on English Marxists was $712.10.

The attempt of the police to cause a riot was called "a disgrace for New York" by one paper. Eleanor, Aveling, and Liebknecht wrote to another, *We have never seen in Europe*

such wanton interference on the part of the police with the
liberty of the subject as we saw today in a country proverbi-
ally known as "the land of the free."

There was no quiet retreat, no time to rest between
speeches and meetings. Tenth Street provided no refuge.
Rosenberg's railroad apartment, one room following the
next, offered little privacy. Tenements were noisy and
preserved the smells, the blood and guts, of each household.
But they soon left for New England, not ever staying long
anywhere else they were to travel. If a movie were to be
made of her American tour, one would see pages fly from
calendars, clock hands spin, and headlines slapped one
on top of the next. The headlines of the *New York Herald,*
for example, read, "Socialist Pleadings. Cooper Union
Crowded. Spurred on by a Woman."

> "In European countries, it took the working class years and
> years before they fully realized the fact that they formed a
> distinct and, under existing conditions, a permanent class
> of modern society; and it took years again until this class-
> consciousness led them to form themselves into a distinct
> political party, independent of, and opposed to, all the old
> political parties formed by the various sections of the rul-
> ing classes. On the more favoured soil of America, where
> no medieval ruins bar the way, where history begins with
> the elements of modern bourgeois society as evolved in the
> seventeenth century, the working class passed through
> these two stages of development within ten months."

Engels also believed in the myth of a new society that
could be molded in a sensible, modern way, without "feudal
traditions or appendages." The Buddekes, however, were to
win.

RETURNING TO New York, Eleanor made notes on the differences between English and American workplaces and
unions. Corporations, banks, and trusts controlled a great

deal and, although machines replaced workers more frequently in America, certain trades, Eleanor wrote, were 50 percent more labor-intensive than in England. American labor politics were complicated and regarded as a "slippery business" by Engels. Workplace observations notwithstanding, for Rosenberg one judgment echoed: New York, shoddy and dirty. Did she fault the landlords or tenants for shoddiness and dirt? It seems obvious she must have known it was the former, but he wished she had said so; after all this remained his city. Rosenberg worked hard to raise the money to have them give the American lecture tour, and he was beginning to be suspicious of Aveling. Eleanor was devoted to him and was blind to all his antics.

In her loneliness Eleanor found no comfort in the geography of New York's Lower East Side. The nearby Tompkins Square Park was dangerous, and walks by herself, Rosenberg told her, were out of the question. Moments alone were limited to climbing his tenement stairs, smelling different cooking smells on each landing. When she reached the apartment she tried to write, but sounds of crying children and raised voices came through the ceiling and walls. She chain-smoked and stopped eating.

Eleanor used to say that she inherited her father's nose and she would one day sue him for damages. She must have seen many similar noses in Rosenberg's neighborhood, but how she felt about the similarity has not been recorded.

THEY TRAVELED to Chicago by train. Aveling eyed hats and legs in the dining car, both fascinated and repelled by what he perceived as flat accents. He was collecting notes for a book of random observations, a Thackeray-like sketchbook, called *An American Journey*. He observed that American women spoke and chewed gum simultaneously and took generous amounts of snuff. Under the pretext of research he spent hours trying to observe a woman "hiding" snuff. He also observed that Americans wiped their noses on their sleeves, employed spittoons, and had poor aim.

They were coarse, money-grubbing provincials.

One of the myths Eleanor would speak against was the idea that socialists wanted to have women in common, and the men who made these accusations, she said, were not workers but owners of the means of production anyway. Chicago was in a state of siege in the aftermath of the Haymarket trial. The Chicago Eight, anarchists unfairly tried and convicted, had been sentenced to hang. The Chicago press warned of "Dr. Aveling and his vitriolic spouse" in the language of a carnival sideshow. The anarchist paper *Frieheit,* in opposition to the Marxists, thought Eleanor should have been shot on sight upon arriving. Yet they drew huge crowds and all their meetings seemed a success.

AVELING PREFERRED actresses, but they were more difficult to locate once he left New York, and he looked down on what passed as theater in America, although he admired Buffalo Bill's Wild West Show. He made no secret of what he thought of as the poverty of American culture. His disdain was a source of embarrassment to his sponsors, but a greater embarrassment developed as they prepared to return to London.

He developed an aphorism, *New York is over-eager to get rich,* and he repeated it constantly, goading Rosenberg.

Rosenberg's suspicions of Aveling multiplied as piles of receipts were turned in. He had demanded exorbitant fees for his speaking engagements and billed the Socialist Labor Party for theater tickets and corsages which he claimed were for Eleanor. The irony of excessive expenses incurred for Karl Marx's daughter wasn't lost on Rosenberg, but Aveling called his accusations ridiculous, and he was defended from England by Engels who brushed off Aveling's embezzlements as the pranks of a boyish "noodle." Rosenberg could sense the counter-accusations ringing across the Atlantic, the worst of them perhaps unspoken: Americans had idealistic and somewhat puritan expectations of how Dr. Aveling should have behaved, Americans are a simple people, literal-minded and dependent on secondary sources of information.

London papers in fact ate up the scandal, writing that the New York socialists would "nevermore import a professional agitator from the effete monarchies of Europe. The luxury is too expensive." When questions about the contradictions between his enormous lecture fees and his supposed interest in the disenfranchised, Aveling replied, *Well, it's English you know, quite English.*

WHEN ELEANOR left, the Statue of Liberty had just been unveiled in New York harbor: icon for future paperweights, imitation foam tiaras, and flashlights covered with foam flames, an image to be printed on bumper stickers, T-shirts, and sweatpants, some of which, through donations, will find themselves passed out by evangelical missionaries in Central America one hundred years after the unveiling. But in 1886, when Eleanor Marx sailed back to England, the statue was a symbol in its infancy, a giant thing, a gift from France, constructed in parts and shipped across the Atlantic.

4

IF YOU WALK east from the Telephone Bar and Grill, you arrive at the block where Eleanor Marx stayed when she came to New York. The buildings are the same as they were one hundred years ago; there has been no development on this block. Crack dealers operate on the west end of the street, near the Good Medicine and Co. storefront theater. The Russian-Turkish baths are directly opposite 261 East Tenth Street and were probably there when Eleanor Marx spoke in New York. They reserve only one day for women, but in 1886 there may have been no day reserved for women at all. Two sixty-one is between a reggae music store, which has T-shirts and records in its window, and the Osgood Fulfillment House, a halfway house for runaway children.

Cooper Union is a few blocks west. In front of the building people sell junk either stolen or scavenged from the garbage. They have bundles and shopping carts full of things, old magazines, books, used clothing, shoes. When it rains they huddle against the building, leaving the objects on blankets or broken-up cardboard boxes, only to return to selling when the rain stops. The park behind the school is full of homeless people who have set out their blankets and mattresses near the statue of Peter Cooper. There is a methadone clinic nearby and on Saturday morning, if it's raining, junkies, too, meet under the Romanesque arches. Lately none of these groups have been present in the park, but as it gets warmer they will return.

5

ON A LONDON bus she had heard a driver announce Stoke–Jewington when driving through Islington. She had heard rhyming slang, she knew what *four by twos* meant, and she'd once been asked if she could speak with a Jewish accent. The man had come up to her at the entrance to the library where she worked and just asked her. *Can you speak with a Jewish accent?* She thought he might have meant a New York accent, but she was from Los Angeles and wouldn't have tried anyway. She'd also been addressed near Notting Hill Gate in Arabic. When she couldn't answer, the man turned to his friend and said in English, *She's not one of ours.*

At work everyone was talking about the television dramatization of the original Jack the Ripper story. Michael Caine played a highly emotional, fairly hard-drinking detective who finally uncovered the queen's physician as the Ripper.

"Did you know he was Jewish?" someone asked.

"The queen's physician?"

"No, Michael Caine."

The head librarian expressed incredulity. Judy Holliday, Piper Laurie, Laurence Harvey, Cary Grant (half), a woman in the cataloging department who claimed to be Polish, those he knew about, but Michael Caine? He said he was going to start a Secret Jew of the Week Club. A different one would be selected each week, but entries would have to be believable. The Prince of Wales was out, and so on. It was funny for a while but the novelty soon wore off. It was hard to top Michael Caine, and later the woman confessed she wasn't even sure about that one.

6

IN NEW YORK in 1882 I met Oscar Wilde. After lectures, theater openings, at private parties, I would infiltrate his circle, usually posing as a reporter or a photographer, and while he tried to snub me, I pretended to ignore his ignoring me. It was difficult to see him alone, but I did manage a few times. I knew that my presence annoyed him, but if I'd stop to nurse hurt feelings, I'd travel home each night on the el, lonely and defeated, in the way one can be on a train. So I just barged on. I made my way home each night with at least some notion of hope and plans for a new assault on Wilde. With what little money I had I would try to wear unusual suits or hats, learning a combination of subtlety and the unexpected in order to gain attention. After leaving me outside a restaurant in the theater district while he and his friends dined inside with Oliver Wendell Holmes or P. T. Barnum, I realized it was stupid to pander to his interest in aesthetics. I was neither an aspiring poet nor actor and had never been further east than Brooklyn. I wanted to offer him something no one else would. One night as he waited for a young man to find him a cab, I saw my chance. He was alone for just a few minutes and I made my offer.

"Oscar," I said, "let me take you to Coney Island, it's like Brighton, I think, the Brighton of the New World." I really had no idea if this was true.

He wasn't interested.

"Oscar," I tried again, "after engaging in a critique of American culture in speech after speech, will you fail to visit the spot where Walt Whitman had been known to read Homer and Shakespeare to the waves?"

He became mildly interested. I nearly told him Coney Island was also known as Sodom by the Sea, but thought better of it. Some subjects, I'd learned during the weeks I followed Oscar Wilde, were better left only as implications.

We arranged to take the train out on a Saturday. I knew Oscar would have preferred a quieter, less raucous venture, on a weekday perhaps, but I had to work during the week. You know, Oscar, I have a job, it's just one of those things, I said. On the train as we rode past the spines of Manhattan to the flat rooftops of Brooklyn, he told me something of his travels in North America, indeed, he had been much further west than Jersey City, even beyond Chicago. He told me how he had been deceived by a young man who claimed to be the son of a banker, and he had lost money in a gambling casino because he believed the con artist. It had been a narrow escape, and I was impressed. He had next invested in Kelly's Perpetual Motion Company and lost more money. In one city he had been impersonated by a woman named Helen Potter, and in another a boy of sixteen managed to get into his hotel room. He'd left school and wanted his advice on becoming a writer. I just gave him a piece of fruit, Oscar said, and told him to learn French. Yeah, I'll bet, I thought.

I was curious about Kelly's P. M. Company. Was it to do
with zoetropes or physical fitness? Afraid to ask seemingly
stupid questions, I kept my mouth shut. At about high noon
we arrived at Coney Island and approached the boardwalk.
People pushed and shoved, stared at his madder lake suit,
trousers cut off at the knee. He looked faintly uncomfortable and began to sweat. I pointed to the bathing lockers
where we could leave our things and go for a swim. No, he
shuddered. Wrong again, I realized, of course Oscar Wilde
wouldn't swim with the immigrant masses. I had the sinking
feeling of failure.

Look, I pointed to the site of the former Coney Island
House. Do you know who used to stay there? Melville and
Edgar Allan Poe.

"Together?" he asked.

The day, though hot, seemed more promising. We took a
long walk down the Iron Pier. Oscar took his jacket off and
I offered to carry it for him. It would have been easy to nick
his wallet at that point. The crowd was full of pickpockets,
as I pointed out to him, and I could have easily said, Well,
I am sorry, Oscar, but you know it is one of the risks here. I
bought him a red hot, a sort of sausage on a roll with mus-
tard. He wouldn't eat it, so I did. Later when he was hungry,
he ate three of them in a row, washed down with bottles of
beer which he said he didn't much care for. American beer,
pooh. The Atlantic Ocean splashed against the pier, and he
stared out to sea and began quoting Homer. A few people
stared. Coney Island is about staring, and he seemed to
enjoy being a spectacle even for dirty children with candy-
smeared mouths. He was invisible here, just a man in a
strange suit and a funny accent. Some mimed dances and
twirled around him, humming popular songs. Little did
they know this was the fellow for whom "The Flippity Flop
Young Man" was written, and I wasn't about to tell them.
Would it have made any difference if I had? Did he enjoy

being a temporarily anonymous spectacle, or did he believe these seamstresses and pipe fitters knew who he was? I couldn't quite tell, and as a sort of curator of the afternoon, it made me nervous. One woman pointed to his madder lake trousers, said she wouldn't mind a pair like those. Oscar didn't pay any attention to her.

By late afternoon we'd stopped in at a number of bars along the pier. I managed to keep boys away from him, but in one alley he disappeared. It was the Bowery, I think, the worst of all Coney Island's dark corners, and I ventured down it, calling his name and looking in dirty windows. It occurred to me that he might well have heard me and decided not to answer. I still had his jacket, but he had taken his wallet out at one of the bars and had that with him.

It was growing dark as I walked down the pier alone, his jacket draped over my shoulders, and I wondered if I should really look for Wilde at all. He could find his way back to New York somehow. He could speak English. He could ask directions. I sat on the shore and stared at all the junk left on the beach: beer bottles, paper wrappers, bits of clothing, shreds of cigarettes. I thought I saw something purple floating in the tide, a pair of trousers, or a skirt, an upside-down umbrella even. In the twilight and without my glasses, I couldn't really tell. Would I one day show people this jacket and say that it had been a lovely afternoon in Central Park when he gave it to me and, in closing, would I say that after he disappeared into the trees, I never saw Oscar Wilde again? The purplish thing drifted onto the beach, but I felt too lazy to walk over and examine it. The stars were clouded over, the gaslights were dim, then grew a bit brighter, and I could hear a tinkly organ out of tune, coming from the direction of the Iron Pier. Perhaps he thought I was the impersonator, dressed as a man, hoping to win his confidence and thus learn the kind of mannerisms and opinions he might reveal only in private. Perhaps he thought that, and he'd given me the slip.

I brushed sand from my suit and strolled toward the pier, stepping on a rotten orange. I nearly slipped on the convex peel as it made a squishing sound underfoot, doing small damage to my shoe. The Bowery looked ominous but I wasn't afraid. It was time to make some attempt to look for him.

7

FINALLY WE give in and rent the movie we ignored a few months ago when we went to see *Midnight Run.* As we listen to Kevin Kline run through every possible cliché about the English, people who live upstairs begin to fight. The noise gets louder and louder, and we wonder if they are beating their children. *You think you have balls? Well my balls are bigger than your balls.* Father to eleven-year-old son. Sound of slaps. John Cleese tells Jamie Lee Curtis he doesn't like being English all that much. It's a pain being so repressed, he more or less says. I call the police and describe the sounds of the fighting going on above my head. It's Saturday night and they may not come. Sometimes they do, sometimes not. We could turn up the volume, but it doesn't help. Before it ends, we rewind and just wait. A brain-damaged man who lives with his mother near the top of the tenement comes in at eleven o'clock, after sweeping out Seventh Street Pizza. He always repeats certain phrases over and over. Sometimes it's *No news is good news. No news is good news. I always say, no news is good news.* Tonight it's the story of his uncle and as he stands around in the hall, he talks about his Uncle Rocco who was stationed in Ipswich. His uncle was fond of french fries, and he tells the empty corridor for the hundredth time that they are called chips over there, and they are eaten with vinegar. *Normandy Beach,* he repeats as he climbs the stairs. *Normandy Beach. Normandy Beach,* as if it's a man's name: Norman D. Beach. His mother interrupts his reverie, yelling down the stairs, asking where the hell he thinks he is. "You're in New York, you know. It's not D-Day either." The corridors are quieter as he climbs the stairs. He yells up that he's never heard of D-Day. What is she talking about? "And you never will," his mother yells back. Ipswich is something like the mural of Naples in one of the pizza places he sweeps, foreign and unimaginable, but he knows it's the middle of the night, and it's time to get to the top floor or his mother's yelling will never end. As he climbs the stairs everyone in the building hears his monologues about a place he's never seen and whose existence is really only a rumor or a joke laid on him by an Uncle Rocco who may never have been there either.

Aedicule

My humor resembles that of Cromwell. I also owe much to Christopher Columbus, because the American spirit has occasionally tapped me on the shoulder and I have been delighted to feel its ironically glacial bite.

—Eric Satie

Does the glacial American spirit resemble the doughboy monster at the end of *Ghostbusters,* a creature capable of administering the sort of tap on the shoulder that floors you? Or is the ironic bite characterized by something that's not really funny at all? When the rate of snowfall constantly exceeds the rate of melting, and, on top of it all, the mass begins to move, you might be witnessing a *période glaciaire:* the Ice Age. What does this have to do with fifteenth-century pratfalls? What kind of jokes did Columbus make that could be called distinctly American rather than Portuguese or Italian, and how did Satie get hold of them? Or, more to the point, what are the dangers of taking a forerunner of Dada at face value? How is telling a story like following a map?

Satie looked over his shoulder and viewed each contact with human hand through misanthropic squint. He wrote short titles: "Irksome Example" and "Disagreeable Despair," "*Memoires d'un amnesiaque.*" His titles don't mean literally what they say. He went through periods of complete silence and poverty, feeling betrayed, refusing to compose at all, agreeing only to play anonymously in a Montmartre bar, then going home late at night kicking bottles down the street.

A SMALL coastal town where colonial settlers had landed
grew firecracker wings when summer arrived. The sky was
full of kites and the rebuilt piers were full of radios. In the
middle of the day the glare from the ocean was unusual, and
a view of the pier, seen from above, would reveal a crowd
in uniform: sunglasses, like plastic horseshoes, perched on
everyone's nose, and hot pink or yellow flip-flops clopped
on the slats. My classmates and neighbors were among the
crowd, or they worked behind bars or hopped between
tables in T-shirts and white aprons, the name of the restaurant silk-screened over a pocket or across the back. I had
a day job sitting in a wooden booth handing out brochures,
giving directions to historical sites. Some of my friends had
jobs in the replica colonial village and, dressed as pilgrims,
they trekked out each day to tiny houses smelling of ply-
wood where until half past five they reenacted spinning,
weaving, or forging horseshoes before crowds of children.
Others were lifeguards, sailing instructors, waitresses, clam
shuckers.

At night on one end of "Fisherman's Wharf" a blue neon
clam opened and shut by degrees: Captain Jack's Clam-
house. On the next pier, Jaws, a Mexican restaurant owned
by a Boston entrepreneur, competed. Against its front wall
of weathered clapboard he'd installed a giant mechanical
shark whose wired canvas jaws and mirrored teeth opened
and shut with hungry regularity until someone tending bar
inside slipped and fell on the cord. I stuck my hand into its
mouth feeling safe, the jaws frozen midbite, until they were
plugged in again. A man laughed at me. I looked around for
the source of the voice but the pier was deserted. Thin
mariachi music spilled onto the boardwalk, drowned out by
the sound of high tide surf, just as the smells of chili and
salsa were overcome by the ocean. Invisible Mexican dish-
washers and cooks worked in Jack's as well as in Jaws.
Behind screen doors round the back in hidden kitchens,

they gutted, skinned, filleted and smoked, covered with lemon juice, parsley, and sauce. Knives and lit ends of cigarettes flashed, and the sound of Spanish became a sign of privacy, a language associated with what was eaten but not seen. In both restaurants kitchens were separated from dining areas either by swinging doors or by a wall with a long slot cut into it behind which hot red lights could be seen or a cook's hand might be glimpsed leaving a plate for a waitress as an order of oysters at Jack's or an order of burritos at Jaws was carried away by a college student to a table with a view of the Atlantic.

When they came on their shift, the waiters and waitresses sat at one table eating an early dinner and the kitchen workers sat at another. They didn't or couldn't speak to each other except to repeat the items on the menu once the evening rush began. *Fried clams, chili rellenos, bluefish with slaw, two orders of chicken mole extra guac.*

AT NIGHT the pier is deserted. Through the slats of the boardwalk, plastic bags, wads of tin foil, and Styrofoam cups float in the water. Garbage collector: another summer job.

DURING THE day I sat in my tiny wooden house full of souvenir maps and brochures donated by the Chamber of Commerce. House-shaped, but not a real house, it didn't contain enough space if you were over five feet tall and decided to lie down on the floor. You would knock your head against one of the walls. There was barely enough room to sit without banging your knees against the counter. Most of the time I stood. This was the place where I worked. No one lived here. No one could live in the brochure-and-guide house, but one morning I unlatched the door to find a man sleeping curled up, head resting on a box of maps. The padlock lay at his feet; I'd forgotten to fasten it the night before.

Hey, mister.

He opened his eyes and leaned on his elbow.

¿Es su casa?

I didn't know what to say. He smiled, standing as if to make room for me so we could both huddle in the ridiculous space. I took a few steps in, unshuttered the window, and laid maps in neat stacks on the counter. He reached up and knocked on the sloping roof, then pushed his hands against the walls as if he were Samson. I told him I had to get to work, *My house isn't a real house, you can see that.* I don't know if he understood *not a real house.* I tried to explain by miming the gesture of handing out maps, but my movements looked as if I were dealing a card game, and he responded by imitating a throw of dice. I handed him a colonial brochure. He looked at the picture of a man in a large black hat about to pound a horseshoe balanced on an anvil, then without saying a word he folded the paper, put it in his back pocket, and walked toward the piers.

The day wore on. Cars drove up, dropped off kids who collected maps and guides, then drove off to the colonial village or parked in town so their occupants could eat on the pier. I knew what time everything in town opened and what time everything shut down. If no one was watching I sat perched on the counter, back to the road, swinging my feet against the wall. What would it be like to sleep here? I'd never thought of it.

I watched a woman from a far end of the island arrive, set up her watercolors against a parking lot wall, and sell lighthouses, beaches, and gulls. While she dozed in a folding chair a man in a blue leather jacket sold small lumps in plastic bags and tin foil out of his car trunk; the bags would later find their way to the pier to be sold again or float empty under the boardwalk. At noon I locked my house and bought my lunch at a stand, fried clams and soda, walking as far down the shore as forty-five minutes would allow. I wanted to swim to Penzance or the Scilly Islands, I wanted oysters that slide cold down your throat, but my family didn't eat at Jack's in the middle of the day and never entered Jaws at all. When I returned to my closet-size house, I faced the sun and counted out-of-state license plates if I grew bored.

LATE AT NIGHT after everything had closed, I went back to the beach, snapping artificial diamonds like headlights on my ears, but everyone I knew had gone home. It was the middle of the night, but the giant neon clam still opened and shut. In the sea at high tide were sharks Thoreau made fun of, electric eels, barracuda hiding behind a tangle of six-pack holders. Some people were sitting on the rocks. A few faces turned in my direction, laughing, but no one I knew from school was sitting on the shore facing Spain. I never saw them go swimming, but I did see the man who had slept in my booth. He recognized me, calling *Isabelle, Isabelle* over the rocks. I always left my name tag in the booth, sticking the pin into the wood each night before I left. *Welcome to . . . My name is Isabelle.* He smelled of fish, a man who skewered shrimp, stabbed crabs and pulled off their legs. The neon clam blinked into the night. *Why did they come?* people at school would ask. *Because the streets were made of gold and you could get rich just by being smart for three minutes.*

I handed him the key to my house-shaped booth so he could sleep in it any time, and I pointed to my watch. *Nine o'clock. As long as you leave by nine.* He had a silver Virgin around his neck, and then he pulled them out of his pocket, wrapped in a thin cardboard box, printed with a picture of a man and woman before a beach at sunset. He held his hand toward me, then pointed up the beach toward the parking lot. I made a gesture of sleeping and shook my head. *You can sleep in my house. Where I work. I live in a different house. You can sleep in the place I work.* It's a little house, an aedicule, a cupola on the ground, a pergola, an ideograph of a house, a sign, a symbol, but not a real house. My booth with its sloping roof was houselike in the way a table a child covers with a sheet becomes a house when he or she sits cross-legged under it. *Not a real house. I don't sleep in it.* He took my key and walked up the beach toward the parking lot.

ON SUNDAY morning their families sat on the beach apart from everyone else. Little girls in fluffy pink dresses stood on the rocks, long black braids down their backs. Beer bottles stuck in the sand like a school of bottle-nosed fish beached overnight. A boy ran over the rocks to poke a stick into a tidal pool. He ignored me as I walked past him, my tracks pressed in sand in a direction away from the shore and toward town. The tour guide bureau was open on weekends, and I needed to tell them I'd lost my key.

In a white office with a ceiling fan, and the radio tuned to a station which promised solid Elvis for one hour, Mrs. Janet leaned over the counter and handed me another key without asking any questions.

Don't wear your diamonds, Isabelle. It gives visitors the wrong impression.

They aren't real.

It doesn't matter. Leave them at home.

She squashed a cigarette and turned off the radio as if to prove cigarettes, Elvis, and big diamonds were finished. Neither the director of public relations nor her secretary knew I found occasional signs that someone was sleeping under the sloped roof of the information booth. The brochures showing illustrations of Wampanoag Indians hunting salmon with torch and spear or dipping baskets into rivers to pull out dozens of smelts were in disarray as if they'd been used as a pillow. Outlines of shoes had been scuffed against one of the walls.

At night in Jack's and Jaws I watched the busboys. New ones cleared plates too soon, anxiously refilling water glasses

as if their jobs depended on a brimming cup. A plate fell
to the floor; a manager or waitress yelled over the music,
heads turned, then eating resumed. My sister dropped her
fork and was given another, and my mother, looking out the
window at the tide, said it would grow cold soon. I wanted to
walk out of Jack's and never return.

Don't include me in any of this.

What? my mother said. My sister rolled her eyes as if to
say I was off my rocker again. I could go sit in my booth, but
at night it was no longer mine. There weren't too many days
left. The little house would be boarded up after Labor Day,
fliers and maps left in Plexiglass holders so the few visitors
who came to town could help themselves.

HURRICANE WARNINGS marked the end of the summer. Gale
winds came early. The radio warned, the television warned,
neighbors and shopkeepers boarded windows and filled old
basement fallout shelters with canned food and kerosene
lanterns. The tour guide bureau telephoned: *Isabelle won't
be needed. Someone will be sent to board up in the morning.*
I ran out to the beach, close to dawn, a red dawn like the
illustration on the thin cardboard package, but as the sun
rose the only smacking couples left on the shore were limpets
and jellyfish. I knocked on the door without realizing it was
padlocked from the outside. There was no answer. *You have
to leave before someone comes to seal up this place.* Turning
the key, I could see my breath in the air. The house was
empty, but a note addressed to me lay on the floor written on
one of the road maps. The key had been slipped under the
door, and he'd left me his watch.

On the pier the man from Boston was taking down his
mechanical shark, wrapping body and fins in a large sheet of
plastic and bundling it into the back of a van. Waves were
beginning to pound at the pilings, and in a threatening voice
he asked me what I wanted as if he suspected I might be a

scout for vandals. I showed him the note, but he said he didn't speak Spanish. Jaws would be closed until the end of the hurricane season. He didn't know where anyone was.

I wanted to know what he'd written, but I couldn't ask anyone at school to translate the note. I didn't want them to know its meaning even if as a consequence I huddled under am umbrella of ignorance. I wouldn't want to be the butt of anyone's jokes; in other words, to slide, as Satie imagined, down the slippery slope of Columbus's dry-eyed pranks. I was afraid once the note was translated I would be tapped on the shoulder by the doughboy, a practical joker, a figure who thrived on canned guffaws. *Dipsomaniacs,* I thought of my classmates who'd snicker, *knuckleheads.* There's something ominous in the Coney Island laughing boy whose gaping mouth you pass through on the way to the amusement park, and ice-bound reefs of understanding seem very distant indeed. I kept the watch although it didn't work. My mother would ask, *What's this?,* about to throw it in the trash if I didn't answer; but I would think of something to tell her until I left home, and then it was lost.

Doubling

Before Claudia, an American, met Pierra Chiari, she knew that her cousin had bleached blonde hair, lived in Florence, and had been fired recently from a restoration project in a church or museum, she wasn't sure which, and didn't care that much about the answer. When she and her mother went to meet Pierra at the airport, her mother ducked out of the responsibility of looking for her cousin by complaining about the crowds and confusion at the baggage terminal which would provoke her into an irritable mood, and so she left Claudia to sit by herself in an airport restaurant, a narrow lounge with a baseball game buzzing on an overhead television. While Claudia looked for a blonde woman in a black coat and red scarf she knew her mother would smoke and fume about excessive favors demanded and other favors not returned by family members who'd barely corresponded with them in years. Reading between the lines of infrequent letters it was clear they thought Americans were idiots made of money, while her mother had no doubt they were cunning and deceitful Europeans, condescending and degenerate; but each branch of the family could use the other and would, given even a partial opportunity. Pierra was being sent to New York for an unspecified reason; she was probably running away from someone or hiding something. Her mother decided to foist the visitor off on Claudia, who lived in the city in a railroad apartment where she could be less of a threat and could do less damage than she would be capable of as a spy in a house in Queens.

She predicted Pierra would be late, and she was. When Claudia saw her standing a few yards from the revolving baggage terminal she was tapping her foot against two black canvas bags while studying faces in irritation as if someone had abandoned her. When she saw Claudia her anger dissolved into relief which seemed spontaneous and unrestrained, and Claudia was easily taken in by Pierra's apparent delight at finding her. They collided. It was a pleasurable sensation to be wanted by a stranger, even a stranded and impatient one. Her cousin explained everything twice, first in Italian and then in English. Immigration had not understood what she answered for occupation. They searched her bags. It took forever. Claudia shrugged and told her it didn't matter although in fact, despite her curiosity about Pierra, a small debit had already been lodged on one side of a ledger headed manners and consideration. She studied the black lines around Pierra's eyes that pointed toward her temples, lines that crackled when she smiled, and knew she would have to try to get to the bathroom first in the morning or the day would be lost.

She guided Pierra toward the lounge where they found Claudia's mother talking to a man whose hands rested on a belt buckle with his name on it. Her mother seemed anxious to dodge him, and so made an extravagant show of emotion when the two of them appeared, leaving her admirer at the bar. Claudia knew her mother was far from delirious about having Pierra dumped in her lap, and to Claudia's further irritation, her mother, in a demonstration of transparently artificial enthusiasm, also said everything twice and loudly, in English and in Italian, as if Claudia were both deaf and a dimwit.

"You look so alike," her mother said.

Claudia failed to see any striking similarity between them. Her mother began to speak quickly and in dialect. Claudia couldn't understand all of what she said, but she imagined

an introduction which explained her behavior in an unflat-
tering and revealing light. "My daughter can be difficult,
prone to silence and sulking for no reason I've ever been
able to figure out, but she's really very happy to have you
stay with her."

Claudia lifted one of the black canvas bags which felt as if
weighted down by marble blocks, and they walked, Pierra
and her mother arm in arm, toward the parking lot.
Claudia, watching a man struggle with a crying child, barely
listened to them. A Yankees cap blew past. Pierra disen-
gaged herself to pick it up.

"Pierra will be impatient to see Manhattan," her mother
said in English. They had reached the curb, and Claudia
knew this statement was meant to be a kind of verbal push
out the door, a sign that her mother was bored already and
anxious to get back to work. She accepted a wrapped package from Pierra, as if that were her cue in a scene prompted
by a code of manners and tribute; here was the gift which
enabled her to return to her office. If Pierra noted that she
hadn't been immediately asked to the house, that she was
being brusquely handed to a minion and rushed off to the
city (even if it was a more desirable destination), she didn't
give any sign. Her mother appeared gracious and congenial,
but underneath her welcoming advances lay unbridled suspicion. She wasn't sentimental about family ties, convinced
in her bitter and intractable way that her relatives could
only, somehow, somewhere along the line, be up to their old
tricks. With each intrusion they made she kept thinking,
what do they want from me? How much money do they want
to borrow? What are they going to make me responsible for
now? Claudia wondered if there were some abstract debt on
their side that kept her in their clutches, and what exactly
was the nature, the makeup of those clutches? She wouldn't
be surprised if the debt and the grip Pierra's family had on
them turned out to be entirely imaginary. When her mother

announced that she would return to her office in a real estate company, Claudia wanted to imitate Frankenstein's lumbering walk, saying " 'Friend, good,' you know?" but recognized that no amount of fooling around would convince her mother of anything. She had probably tried to sell the man in the lounge a house. They parted outside the airport, each traveling on to different places.

From the cab Claudia pointed out the Empire State Building and Grand Central Station and found herself making simple statements about obvious facts, "No snow yet. Later, maybe, probably, yes." Reduced almost to lumps of baby-talk as if speaking to a child, Claudia faltered and finally stopped talking altogether. If her mother was to be believed, she wasn't just talking to an adult who had a child's knowledge of the English language, but to a crafty child, one capable of achieving its needs and desires in roundabout but effective ways. A messenger on a bicycle crashed against their cab with a thud. As he fell his face pressed against the window, almost cracking it, nose, cheek, and one eye squashed suddenly and violently against the glass like someone had thrown mashed potatoes at them. He righted himself, then rode on. Pierra jumped at the startling sound, but the continual effort to converse was too much for Claudia. She remained silent, hoping Pierra would do whatever she had come to the city to do and leave her alone. She didn't want the responsibility of looking after anyone. Pierra stared out the window at plumes of steam rising from manholes. A man in a helmet with a light attached to it emerged from one, looking startled and blinking.

CLAUDIA WORKED as an artist in the city court system, selling her drawings to television networks and newspapers. Along with the press and other people anxious to see celebrity trials, she waited in halls outside courtrooms, often behind police barricades. She would arrive early with her inks, portfolio, and special magnifying lenses, binocular-like, that fit over her regular glasses. In the hall, sometimes sitting on the floor while waiting to be let in, she listened to journalists talk about flying in from Moscow, flying out to Egypt, interviewing terrorists and gun runners, interviewing former National Security Council renegades. *You can get to him. After the pardon he went into the bulletproof vest business, calling the company Born Again, Born Again Something. If you tell him you represent a company that will import them he'll talk to you.* Others were more salacious. These, the rumpled chasers of the dethroned and the defrocked, hustlers of newly minted celebrities or revarnished scandal, exhibited a different kind of cynicism. Their suits were vague, cheap imitations of the suits they pursued; they wrote notes on their cuffs. Unwashed or dapper, flying from celebrity trial to war zone, from one interview to the next, all of them spoke with urgency and importance, and while she listened to them Claudia herself felt anonymous and trivial, a handmaiden to the public's voyeuristic desire to see the defendant.

Reduced to waiting around courtroom corridors, leaning against walls, popping Juicy Fruit into their mouths if they weren't allowed to smoke, they, the panderers as well as those with a mission and those with nothing more pressing than a job to do, would eventually be permitted to attend the trial. The crowd who waited only for a partial glimpse of notoriety in the form of an actor, murder witness, or star informant might grow fractious and pushy, but it was tough luck for them. It didn't matter where she stood in line, Claudia had her identification and was always allowed in with the journalists. Once inside she had a designated place to sit. The characters she drew didn't do much beyond talking, passing photographs, articles, video and audio tapes all docketed as evidence. Sometimes she felt herself slipping toward caricature and away from verisimilitude, exaggerating chins, noses, mouths. The settings were always the same.

The yellowed courtroom paint was peeling. The window shades were ripped and dangled ineffectually, letting gray light in. Noise from construction threatened to drown out lawyers and those in the witness box. She enjoyed the ripples that went through court when an unanticipated witness appeared under fluorescent lighting, but such occasions were rare.

Claudia used to paint at night when she came home from work but had given it up. After a day of murders, custody battles, extortion, racketeering, kidnapping, and blackmail, the question of what to draw eluded her. Rows of sharpened pencils and drawing paper offered no shoehorn into possible content. Sometimes she drew words across the page, sometimes she cut pictures out and glued them near the words. She used to make constructions, sometimes in shallow boxes, and all the objects in them had an associative connection: a torn corner of a letter, an X-ray fragment of a tooth, a plastic Cleopatra painted black. They suggested unfolding stories, but she no longer knew what to do with the drawings when they were finished, and the fragile, fragmented surfaces held together with pieces of tape and drops of glue soon fell apart. In museums and galleries, Claudia felt overwhelmed by precedent, even if the precedents were only a few minutes old and still wet. She could no longer explain what she was trying to do and felt increasingly paralyzed when she faced her empty apartment after work. She could see only the accused and the victim. Every possible innate object seemed to fall into one of those two categories. Having Pierra around made her uncomfortable, as if her paralysis were under surveillance, but not only did Pierra watch Claudia, she demanded that she be watched as well.

Claudia's apartment was situated in such a way that no one could see into it. She lived on the top floor of a five-story building, but the surrounding tenements were even lower. The only structures which rose any higher and might have offered a view were boarded-up buildings once lived in, now abandoned. From the top of one a peeling billboard sprouted which hadn't been papered over in years, and, advertising the nerve and perspicacity of a local television news team in dated clothing, it contributed to the landscape of rooftops headed toward the Williamsburg Bridge. Observing the absence of visual access, Pierra began to walk around naked at all hours. Claudia didn't read this gesture as a sybaritic sign or an indication of laziness but as an aggressive nakedness, overwhelming, and domineering; Pierra's naked walking-around self pushed Claudia against a wall. In response Claudia overdressed and refused to stare. Pierra was relentless. If she needed to make calls about upcoming trials, Pierra wanted to practice her English, which turned out to be surprisingly good and didn't need to be practiced, or she would be on the telephone herself talking loudly to people unknown to Claudia. When she got home from the courts there was no chance of collapsing, of doing nothing. Pierra would want to talk, ask questions, run the coffee grinder.

After the first week, she no longer bought Pierra newspapers from Rome or other things she said she needed. Claudia wanted her to find them for herself.

"Here are bus and subway maps, memorize the telephone number in case you get lost."

At first Pierra did go for walks, but the buildings she designated as landmarks seemed to repeat themselves, and she often became disoriented. The sequence of video rental or music shops, pizza counters, and certain clothing chains seemed to repeat itself over and over.

"In other words," Pierra explained, "a cardboard display of a large animated rabbit is followed by a cardboard display of men with no hair, followed by yellow arches, followed by a row of black trousers on white torsos, headless, then a few blocks away this same series is repeated."

She claimed English words, too, lost the uniqueness of their appearance in textbooks and the precision of their sound on language tapes. American speech seemed like vague waves of sound. She perceived the differences between sequential sentences as being only slight, and therefore, she often misunderstood. Pierra mentally planned sentences in English and finished them in Italian when tenses became too complicated and vocabulary forgotten. Claudia thought this was nothing more than another excuse for not leaving the apartment.

When Claudia asked her exactly what she had done in Florence to get fired, Pierra was evasive. She said she now worked for an art dealer whom she was careful not to name in conversation. She repeated the word *reproductions* twice, but Claudia didn't understand.

"He sells reproductions," she said, "not originals."

She was supposed to stay only a month, but when the money for an apartment of her own was slow in arriving from Italy and wasn't really enough when it did arrive, she stayed on in Claudia's long railroad apartment without, as far as Claudia could tell, working at or on anything. She poked at Claudia's drawings of a defendant in a green jumpsuit, "He looks as if he was sure he was going to get off," and she asked about the picture of a plaintiff pointing to a tape recorder. Claudia didn't want to talk about the case and hoped by reading her sullen expression Pierra would get the message: I want you to leave already. Pierra responded by partially undressing; like the arrogant defendant, her body was her weapon of insult.

Claudia occupied only the middle rooms of the apartment, leaving one of the small rooms at the end of the flat empty. It was a room with one narrow window facing an airshaft, little sunlight ever entered it. A few boxes lay against a wall. Its dreariness didn't deter Pierra when she explained she wanted to use the vacant room to work in.

Claudia could only agree, yet she privately snorted at the idea of Pierra working, as if the very word could only be another setup, another ruse. The telephone rang constantly. Why? Although she was skeptical, Claudia was also taken in, and as she watched Pierra move around the apartment her suspicions contained an element of fascination. Her shirt slipped down around her shoulders, and she pushed her hair back over her head so it looked rumpled in a studied manner. She left her shoes all over the apartment. Claudia picked them up and unbuttoned her shirt so it fell down the same way. Her cousin was a few years older, a little taller, and in spite of her uncertainty of local geography she went about the apartment doing things as ordinary as striking a match against a wall or taking an inventory of Claudia's paints with enviable confidence and self-assurance. Claudia's efforts at deflating this confidence were always deflected.

"So why were you fired?"

"I was the wrong person for the job, but I wanted to work on this restoration project. It meant a lot to me even though I knew it was only a matter of time before I screwed up. I put too much red into a soldier's face, and the red was too bright. I knew it would be. He looked flushed and sweaty when before he had looked like stale bread."

"Why did you do it?"

"I don't know." Even in her confusion and desire to avert humiliation Pierra spoke with authority. "I wanted to see what the red would have looked like just as Correggio had painted it himself, just at that moment when the image was barely on the wall." She swept some dried-out paint tubes off the table and into the trash.

"You don't have to throw anything out. I'll get rid of them when I'm ready to."

Pierra rarely spoke about her family, yet Claudia was certain Pierra's mother would defend her daughter even if she had hopelessly botched the job, while her own mother would side with the supporters of stale bread.

"You'll see. I'm very good at what I do. I'm going to have some things sent here."

CRATES BEGAN TO arrive, and for weeks archaic-looking body parts were scattered around the rooms. Arms and legs leaned against chairs as if waiting for a nonexistent torso. Pierra referred to them as classic body parts, but the fragments refused to assemble themselves neatly into whole objects. There was always something missing. Whatever it was, arms and head or nose and ear, the pieces resisted explanation. Claudia ran her hands over plaster or wax when Pierra was in another room. The studio looked morgue-like, but also like a department store window before clothes were put on the dummies, arms and legs still lying on the floor. Claudia leaned against a wall, flipped off a light Pierra had rigged from the ceiling, and felt the joints where her arm met her shoulder and leg met hip. She thought about the body parts she had seen and drawn in the courtroom: meaty hands, nervous twitching eyes, fat legs encased in tight pants.

The first completed sculpture Pierra showed her was a figure of a monk.

"Savonarola," Pierra said, scratching a date on the bottom of the figure.

Claudia had never heard of him and believed Pierra had made up the name. It sounded like a kind of cigar.

"You'd be surprised how many people will want this," she said. Claudia watched as she deliberately broke the base, repaired it with plaster, then flipped through television channels while it set. After Pierra was asleep, Claudia went into the other room and looked at the monk. The date Pierra had scratched into its base read 1496 in Roman numerals. Plaster dust made Claudia sneeze, and the roughness of the molds to touch made her skin crawl. The next day Savonarola was shipped back to Florence.

Pierra got telephone calls from a man named Ehrlich who lived on Staten Island and spoke to her in Italian. The calls began soon after she arrived and occurred at all hours. They spoke, as much as Claudia could tell when she overheard parts of their conversations, about aging and coloring. At first she thought they were talking about hair; only later did she realize Ehrlich and Pierra were discussing plaster. Pierra often hung up after their discussions, hair and hands whitened by plaster smears, with an air of exasperation and resignation. Claudia moved the telephone into the room which had become Pierra's studio.

PIERRA BEGAN working on a marble statue of Beatrice Cenci, a sixteen-year-old girl who murdered her father in 1599. Francesco Cenci, a wealthy Roman Don Juan, took every opportunity to humiliate and impoverish his children, both sons and daughters, and publicly wished they were all dead. For his second daughter, Beatrice, he reserved special tortures. He kept her imprisoned in his palace, La Petrella, where he walked around stark naked and slept in her bed, intending, he said, to have a child who was both his son and grandson. This was all common knowledge; there were no secrets about the Cenci, Pierra told Claudia, everybody knew what went on in La Petrella. Beatrice and her stepmother failed in an attempt to escape and so plotted the murder of Francesco. After drugging him with opium, they summoned two men to finish him off by driving large nails into his eyes and throat. Then his body was thrown over a parapet, and that was the end of him. The two women weren't suspected at first, but under interrogation the laundress at La Petrella who had washed the bloody sheets expressed doubts about Beatrice's innocence. For months nothing was done, and although they could have escaped, the two women remained in Rome. Eventually one of their henchmen was caught, and his confession led to their unmasking.

"Just like the Menendez brothers in Los Angeles," Claudia said. "Cameras were let into their trial."

Pierra had never heard of them. She went on to explain that Beatrice was tortured by something called "the cord," which meant she was hung by her hair until she confessed. After her confession the pope ordered that she and her stepmother be dragged through the streets of Rome tied to the tails of wild horses until the two women were dead, but before they could be executed there needed to be a kind of mock trial. Ridiculing Beatrice's lawyer for defending her, the pope had no thought of clemency. Having let one recent matricide escape in the case of Paolo Santa Croce, who murdered his mother for money and then got away, the pope was out for blood, not for mercy.

"He didn't want to appear soft on crime."

Pierra repeated the word *soft,* she didn't understand what the word had to do with a murder trial.

"What about the plea of self-defense?" Claudia asked.

There was no chance. Last-minute appeals by influential princes came to nothing, and despite the sympathy for them expressed by the city of Rome, the pope ordered Beatrice Cenci and her stepmother to be executed for the slaying.

Pierra began by tacking up photographs of a reproduction of a similar statue which she referred to as she turned the marble on a small pedestal. In the evening Claudia grew mesmerized, watching Pierra glance at the photographs, then chip away at the block. Many angles appeared to compete in cubistic fragments, but gradually the two began to look identical. Claudia didn't ask her cousin what the purpose of a copy might be. She imagined it was part of an installation which included examples of work appropriated from other artists, a kind of critique of theology, the law, and abusive relationships documented in Renaissance Italy.

"It's a complicated tableau with revolving pieces of sculpture, taped music, and a painted backdrop," Claudia told another artist during a break in a trial. She hoped Pierra would keep the scale small. The apartment was already overcrowded.

CLAUDIA OFFERED to take Pierra to the Museum of Modern Art. "You could see Léger, Braque, Rousseau, Juan Gris, Fluxus documents, Dada prints."

"I'm not interested."

She was openly bored in a gallery full of German neo-expressionist paintings and baffled by blown-up photographs, a woman's self-portraits, transformed by increasingly unusual and dramatic costumes and props. Claudia tried to explain that the photographs were parodying themselves.

"Too cinematic, too theatrical." Pierra walked ahead of Claudia and out the door.

The Metropolitan Museum held more interest for her, but she grew nervous when they reached a room of Greek statues. She asked if they could leave the museum, saying in English that she suddenly felt very ill.

"DO YOU KNOW Alceo Dossena?" Pierra asked, wiping her hands on her shirttails.

"No."

"I mean have you heard of him?"

"No," Claudia said, "I haven't."

"He was a forger. His terra-cotta reliefs were nearly flawless, but he dated one done in 1929 with the Fascist year VII and, as a result, was exposed." She scraped a knife clean against the edge of a plate and prepared to go out.

"What was he doing copying Renaissance portraits when he should have been looking into Futurism?"

Pierra ignored her, leaving Claudia to sweep up plaster dust and marble chips. When she departed to buy a new chisel and order more crates, Claudia called her mother.

"Who was Alceo Dossena?"

"I think he owned the Grotto Nero on Eighth Avenue."

Claudia told her mother she didn't think he had anything to do with a restaurant in New York that closed ten years ago.

HER APARTMENT became transformed. Its walls were covered by photographs cut from art books. Sometimes Pierra projected slides on the walls. Italian audio tapes of a reading from Dante arrived in the mail. Crates smelling of freshly cut wood filled the two front rooms. A pair of broken wine glasses were spray-painted through a stencil onto each crate to signify fragile contents, and an address was stenciled on as well: Desiderio Mendacio, Manifattura di Segno, Firenze. The crates were filled with saints, Mary Magdalens, and Medicis. Once they were shipped out, more fabrication followed. Pierra put a pink streak in her darkening blonde hair and studied books on Tiepolo while sitting on the floor, smoking short American cigarettes.

"Like Kim Novak," she said. A color of hair dye from thirty years ago, it was called champagne pink.

"Have you ever thought about the taste for ham-handed historicism?"

Claudia wasn't sure she knew what Pierra was talking about or where she had picked up *ham-handed.*

"Do you mean nostalgia?" Claudia asked.

"Not at all. I know what nostalgia is. The color of my hair is about nostalgia, and that is not what I mean."

"No, I haven't given much thought to it."

"One hundred years ago in France, there was a craze for medieval ivories. Every bourgeois household had to have them and the demand was far greater than the supply.

Artists who had considered themselves failures became rich overnight fabricating large numbers of fake carvings. I mean, the ivory was real, but the carvings, at the time, were not old. They were stained to look medieval but they were new in 1880. It wouldn't be a bad thing to own one now, one of these forgeries, they would be worth a fortune. Neo-Gothic style presented certain difficulties right off the bat: it was a ready-made imitation, and you had to be careful of anachronism."

Claudia didn't know what she was getting at or where she had picked up the expression "off the bat," either. Perhaps Ehrlich sprinkled his speech with sports metaphors. As her cousin spoke of the problems of molds and casting, Claudia's attention wandered.

Pierra's meticulous statues and deliberately damaged friezes and her black and coral suits from Italian *Vogue* of 1964 made Claudia feel how her own clothes were worn carelessly, fit badly, and all her cuts and bruises were slow to heal. In a defensive moment while touching up a lawyer's hairpiece, she began to wonder if she had confused her cousin's meticulousness with doggedness, and her ingenuity with a simple talent for ferreting out the obscure. Late at night she could hear Pierra carefully amputating the arms and legs of saints and heretics whose names meant nothing to her. The sound of chiseling and chipping was annoying, and she had no idea what kind of people would pay money for these things. If something was smuggled out in the hollow figures, then Pierra was indeed the crafty child, lost but scheming, that her mother was sure they had met at Kennedy months ago.

"DEALERS FREQUENTLY place reproductions in old villas to add to the aura of authenticity. This relieves the anxiety of the buyer. He or she, in a genuinely historic setting, becomes embarrassed to inquire if the pieces are fake. How do you ask without offending everyone in sight? It's impossible."

Claudia had been staring out the window at the billboard and, not wanting to appear rude, didn't ask Pierra if she meant that the practice of planting fakes in old estates was done in Italy now, or if that had been the practice one hundred years ago. The apartment was shrinking from the clutter of crates, packing chips, halves of molds, and marble dust.

"You know, you might discover you need more space. You can still find cheap apartments if you really look."

Pierra ignored her. Claudia regretted the loss of her privacy and felt pushed to the side by Pierra's industry, which threatened to consume her as well. With so many judges allowing television cameras in courtrooms there was less work, and Claudia had more time at home but still had no time to herself.

"I'm going to a midnight show," Claudia said.

"I'm staying here." American movies, she claimed, were still essentially a blur of sounds to her with a few recognizable words and phrases poking through a sea of gibberish. Annoyed at her perfunctory but unequivocal answer, Claudia left quickly. She herself was often ambivalent about even simple things. Unable ever to serve on a jury because of her work, she knew she was incapable of being convinced of a definite verdict in many cases. She waffled, she was too easily swayed. As the door shut behind her and she tilted her head over the railing that resembled lead pipes brought into the city from a firebombed Dresden, she was actually glad to be able to go out alone. The banister spiraled down to bent mailbox flaps; a few could actually lock. What did Pierra think of this place? She didn't know if Pierra would ever go back to Florence or find an apartment of her own. A man, barely visible, his face turned against the wall, slept under the stairs. It was easy to gain access to the building. You pressed all the buzzers until someone let you in. Holding one of Pierra's veiled pillbox hats on her head with one hand, Claudia ran past him.

The movie had already begun by the time she got to the theater. It was a film about a woman who, although she could barely speak English, worked at a censor's office examining different kinds of pornography. While sitting in a screening room she secretly copied the films with a hidden camera, then brought the duplicates home to her sister. Claudia believed there was a relationship between what the woman in the film did and her occupation drawing people on trial. She sat in the empty theater for a few minutes imagining what her job would be like if she had to do it in a country whose language was meaningless to her. Would she be able to guess the kinds of crimes being tried based on visual evidence alone (a stained sheet instead of the testimony of a laundress), or would she rely on sets of universal gestures on the part of lawyers and witnesses (the accusatory finger, the shrug)?

Walking past a group of men clustered around their double-parked cars, a Lebanese bakery which smelled of cardamom and roasting pistachios, a twenty-four-hour laundromat with its manager emptying quarters and lint traps, Claudia easily confused the fatigue of the night shift with early-morning industry. She tried to guess what language the men spoke between themselves and into their car phones. They stared back at her, leaning their hips against black four-door sedans. They considered her to have a provocative body. Annoyed, she moved awkwardly. Getting from one end of the street to the other seemed to take an hour, then she turned around. Claudia didn't want to go home. The apartment full of marble blocks, terra-cottas, endless crates, and heaps of packing chips that seemed to glow in the dark disturbed her as a site of chaos and ghosts.

Finding a cab she went to her mother's house in Queens,

and even though it was three in the morning she telephoned Pierra as soon as she got in.

"You must see that you have to leave. I need my apartment back."

Her mother, woken by the sound of Claudia's entrance, leaned against the kitchen door jamb, her body hidden behind a large T-shirt which read "It's Pleasure to Serve You" over the picture of a coffee cup. She grabbed the telephone. "You can't throw her out in the street, and besides, you need someone to pay half the rent. You never go to work anymore."

"My job stinks."

"*Cosa? Cosa?*" Pierra's voice sounded on the other end of the line.

"Forget it, all I meant was that I'll be back soon."

Claudia wanted to remind her mother about relatives who visited the house of the bereaved after a funeral only to eat, but she said nothing.

"WHY DON'T YOU cut off that arm? I'll pay you."

"How much?"

THE ANONYMOUS dealer in Florence sent them a fax requesting more pieces. Although work was continually sent out, many of the crates never reached him. As demands for replacements increased, shipments continued to get lost. Industrious and undeterred, Claudia polished marble, prepared molds, mixed paint, measured brilliantly powdered pigment into white china bowls. Her sense of color grew more accurate than Pierra's. Her pale ochers and burnt siennas were perfect, and the madder lake she mixed was muted down until it looked like a madder lake that could only have been vivid hundreds of years ago.

"I'm no longer satisfied with having my work bought as copies."

"You mean forgeries." Claudia wanted to know why the sudden discrimination. She shifted in her chair uneasily.

"Artificial originals. I would even accept a made-up identity as long as it was mine alone."

Pushing her own doubts aside Claudia ignored the signs of Pierra's discontent. Questions of identity bored her. In her pragmatism born out of early independence and the need to pay the rent no matter what, Claudia felt they should just get on with it and not worry about vague borders of individuality, theirs or a group of dead men in velvet. They're long departed, she said, forget about it. Pierra's moody posing and complaining, performing as Miss Italian Neo-Realism, was just intentional and messy artifice, unnecessary and superficial. She wanted to say, come off it, will you? A job was what mattered, a job you were well paid for, where you weren't badly treated or compromised, a job well done that you could take pride in. That was all that mattered. Portraits of perjurers, the gypped and the bludgeoned, drawings of lawyers who wore diamond pinkie rings were all in the past, and she was glad of it, more glad than she would ever have believed possible. Pierra, as far as Claudia acknowledged at that moment, had turned out to be all right.

A MONTH LATER they received another fax from the dealer. Many of the lost crates had suddenly turned up in a warehouse in Rome. The work was intact, but the crates themselves had been damaged, addresses partially or entirely defaced. A few had been traced to the dealer, and he had been able to intercede before the works were confiscated, but he had to pretend he knew little about the contents of the crates addressed to him from a city and person whose names were so defaced as to remain (the dealer must have lied) a mystery. A man from the University of Rome was called in to identify the work. After examining their contents under the dealer's nervous eye he declared them to be a lost collection of paintings and terra-cotta pieces by Massimo Cambio, a Florentine artist who died by poisoning in 1868.

"*Chi era Cambio?*" Pierra waved the letter in the air. She read out loud, brokenly translating as she went along. "Many believe Massimo was murdered by his creditors, but the authority from Rome thinks he probably died of lead poisoning."

"How?"

"Licking his brushes so that the ends would point," Pierra translated. "A common death."

Claudia shot a foam packing chip across the floor. It scudded behind a radiator. It would stay there forever. Running oily hands over his head, Cambio left red streaks in his hair. He shuttered his windows. He turned pictures against the walls. He heard his creditors in the courtyard, smelled cheap bones boiling in soup downstairs, and looking at himself in a mirror for what he imagined was a melodramatic last time, he fled over tiled rooftops.

"What do we know about him?"

"Nothing."

His works were popular melodramatic scenes, but they were now rare, and because there were so few of them, they were difficult to identify. As a result of the discovery in Rome, Pierra's hand had been authenticated as that of Cambio. She could produce almost whatever she liked and, within reason, it would be considered the work of this dead man.

"I don't want to be Cambio, condemned and second-rate." She crumpled the letter into a ball. "Why couldn't I be Turner or Velásquez?"

Claudia felt helpless. The tricks of paint and of identity spiraled into something complicated and beyond her. She picked the ball off the floor, smoothed out the pages, and handed it back to her. Pierra continued to read in a kind

of English, saying in Italian the words whose English translation was unknown to her. Cambio, besides being a producer of originals, had also done a little forgery, but even
these copies, clever and easily circulated in Rome, were of
interest.

"Cambio is me. Cambio isn't me," Pierra said. "I don't
want to impersonate a forger." In Pierra's dissatisfaction,
Claudia saw a depth of purpose that had eluded her when
she lived alone, and it terrified her, but she barged on. Impersonate: to take on characteristics of. . . . All right, Pierra
said, superficial work habits maybe, but down to the core?

"Once freed from executing generic period pieces of
anonymous or occasionally specific authorship, you can
have a fairly flexible identity. Cambio could be considered
to be ahead of his time," Claudia suggested. She felt authori-
tative in the face of Pierra's doubts and quaverings. She was
the interrogator who demanded to know where the accused
was on the night of the twenty-fifth, using the full force of
what facts he guessed or was willing to risk were on his side.
Claudia reached for the telephone and ordered take-out
food with conviction. She began to take charge while Pierra
felt reduced, wary, neither entranced nor seduced by the
petty producer of melodramas who suddenly seemed to enter
her life waving his passport and thrusting it into her hands
whether she wanted it or not.

CLAUDIA BOUGHT some old musical instruments found in a
storefront a few blocks from her building. She took them
apart, and Pierra put them back together again incorrectly.
Reassembled with odd bits of bottle labels, postcards, and
flattened forks, the result was vaguely surrealist. Ehrlich
told them about a kind of glue which resisted dating techniques and looked as if it had been applied decades before it
actually had. Cubist and surrealist sculpture, all made to
look painstakingly authentic, were crated up and sent to

Florence. When the dealer received these pieces signed by Cambio, he cabled back that they shouldn't push their luck. Not much was known about Cambio, outside of the gambling debts, but he certainly hadn't been a freakish visionary when he died in Tuscany in 1868. He painted melodramas: contemporary murders, a few crucifixions, a voyeur watching a kiss, pictures of weeping women with sappy titles. His sculptures were no different.

The dealer sent a photograph of a painting called *The Morphology of Revenge,* writing that as far as he knew this was Cambio's ur-painting, the rubric from which all the rest of his narratives sprung. Claudia studied it carefully. One man stabbed another man while others watched from across the street and from windows. Blood flowed in unnatural curves from wounds in the body of a dying man who was supported by a third figure. There was no hint as to what the nature of the dispute might have been or if the picture was based on a true story.

NEW ORDERS arrived from Florence nearly every week, and they considered looking for a larger studio in which to work. Claudia suggested they ask the dealer for higher rates.

"I can't ask for more money."

Claudia was surprised by Pierra's sudden grace. Where had the mercenary instinct, legendary and reliable, flown off to so abruptly? Claudia threatened to withdraw her half of the operation. "I want at least enough so that I never have to go back to court." She wrote a letter outlining their demands, and Pierra translated it into Italian.

Pierra worked slowly. Her attention to Cambio flagged even more; he was not a cathectic object for her, and Claudia's interest remained entirely pragmatic. She had a reason for continuing their new mutual identity, and she egged Pierra on mercilessly. She had no pity for Pierra and no patience with her reluctance or her hesitation, existential and tiresome. She found herself using an excessive number of idiomatic expressions like "take the bull by the horns," which Pierra probably didn't understand. In the mundane images of Cambio's short life—wet brushes placed dangerously near plates of gnocchi hardened into stones, or in overturned glasses of wine licked clean by cats and dogs—Pierra saw vacuity, pettiness, and self-pity. These images repulsed her, but intoxicated Claudia. Cambio represented something elusive, romantic, but most importantly, he freed her from the drudgery of defendants and prosecutors.

"You riddle while Rome burns," Pierra said. Cambio's identity imposed something fixed and burdensome. She felt the project was like trying to reproduce Canaletto's paintings of Venice without a straight edge or a grid. "I don't like him. I know what he was. He was a failure."

THE DEALER wired them more money than they'd asked for. Cambio was doing very well, and so for Claudia, at least, he was redeemed.

Consulting the invisible Ehrlich, she didn't know if he had learned whom they had become, but his calls grew indispensable. Once the work had been authenticated in the cellar in Rome, no one asked any questions, and there seemed to be no shortage of buyers.

"Thermoluminescent testing," Pierra said, "could expose us," tapping an eyelid with the end of a brush.

Claudia continued to ignore her doubts and misgivings. She saw nothing to worry about and only grew more confident as checks arrived on a regular basis. Sometimes she would look at the clock and imagine journalists and artists standing in line outside a courtroom, lingering, smelling the men's room down the hall, feeling pathetic and parasitic, waiting for a serial killer or letter bomber. Laughing at them from the distance of her apartment she mixed intensely bright colors. The dealer no longer sent complaints when terra-cotta friezes arrived painted viridian and scarlet as if Cambio had been a very early fauve.

She pressed her sweaty forehead and handprints against a window. The prints were tinted blue; the mark of her forehead was like a thumbprint through which Claudia could see tenement rooftops stretching to the river.

"Look-alikes," Pierra said, "it happens, sometimes only by accident. When you're a child you think somewhere out in space there is a city just like the one you live in. Down to the smallest detail; the timing of streetlights, the dripping of taps: it's the same. A girl just like you, with parents exactly like yours, lives in the same house with the same smell of turpentine or floor wax, for example, and she is thinking the same thoughts as you. If only the two of you could meet, you would understand each other perfectly."

"Duplicates, not duplicitous," Claudia said, wiping a brush hard against a rag.

Pierra had shown Claudia as many of the techniques of copying as she knew. There had never been a doubt that what they were engaged in was, essentially, trickery and the results were so exact, the dealer had written, the dates no longer mattered.

"It's no longer a question of evidence which can be seen, Pierra, you have to know a particular piece was made in an apartment in New York with a view of a billboard Marlboro Man and '*Perdido*' on the radio. Someone would have to have told you. You, me, the dealer we write to care of Desiderio Mendacio, none of them or us are going to tip our hand, I think. When faced with an original and its copy, anyone, years later, might not know which was which." Dipping a paper towel into turpentine, Pierra wiped her marks off the window, leaving a greasy landscape.

PIERRA CEASED to trust the dealer. She cashed his checks but no longer read his letters and kept them from Claudia.

Everything they knew about Cambio had been learned through him, but Pierra was suspicious. Libraries and museums provided little corroboration. Cambio could have been an invention all along.

CLAUDIA'S MOTHER began to telephone more often. She wanted to know what was going on. Claudia told Pierra that her mother was probably between boyfriends and so had more time to be inquisitive. Where did she find them? Men in waiting rooms, in restaurants, men met in trains as they read the paper, men bumped into while they stood around like dummies reading subway ads to themselves, not to mention clients. The expression on Pierra's face took on the same appearance it had when Claudia guided her past the *Mollusks and Your World* exhibit on the way to the Imax theater at the Museum of Natural History. Abruptly, in light of Pierra's disgust, Claudia felt oddly defensive, and she wanted to tell Pierra that her mother had a right to seduce whomever she wanted to. Whether she was entangled with someone or not, her mother said she wanted to visit them, perhaps take them out to dinner. Pierra looked startled and hacked a hand off a reclining man as if to say this is all your fault, Claudia, you jerk, control her. Again Claudia was miffed.

"What are you afraid of? What's wrong with dinner? She's trying to be nice." The word *nice* stuck, sounded trite, a word larded with excuses, but Claudia meant it.

Still the calls were unexplained and provocative. Why was she so concerned all of a sudden? Or was her concern a ruse behind which she was only planning on the expansion of her real estate listings to include tenements and flophouses?

During one call her mother took Pierra's side, yet she did so without having a clue as to what they did all day. She was sure Claudia was ignoring Pierra, leaving her to sit alone in the apartment, afraid to leave the building. On the other hand she invented a scenario in which Claudia took advantage of her cousin, making her do things, engaging in business transactions, buying drugs for example, a process which a Florentine like Pierra would never understand.

"Don't send her into the streets. She lives in the fifteenth century."

"Fifteenth century? Have you seen the way she dresses?"

"She'll get lost. She won't know what to do or how to speak."

Claudia reminded her mother that she worked in the courts. She didn't traffic in anything illegal. The intimidation in the next call then took a different form. Her mother threatened to call Immigration. Pierra should go back. Pierra was cagey and a bad influence. They were up to something.

"I don't want to visit you in Riker's Island."

"Women aren't sent to Riker's."

"How do you know?"

"Just relax. Everything's fine."

Perhaps because of the phone calls Pierra began to go to the movies with Claudia, unaware that Claudia nervously watched her study the screen. Any story, Claudia believed, might influence her in ways which would interfere with the Cambio project. When Pierra began to use expressions like "fatal attraction," "out of my/our control," and made many references to fate, Claudia grew alarmed. At the same time, she worried about leaving Pierra alone for too long. She watched her as she prepared a terra-cotta frieze to be painted. If her cousin grew homesick, or tired of Claudia and tired of an apartment that she was often afraid to leave, she could fly back to Florence anytime. All Claudia could do was to keep her under an edgy kind of surveillance, as if her watching were either natural or accidental, hoping to stop her from doing anything rash that would end their career as Cambio and send Claudia back to court.

"What are you staring at?" Pierra yelled across the room.

"OK," Claudia yelled back. "I give up. Do us in. See if I care." Claudia tried to stay out of her way for the rest of the afternoon.

After New Year's Pierra finally began to take long walks around the city. She claimed that was what she did, and in conversation, the streets and subways made sense as she referred to them.

"Is it really historicism or sentimental nostalgia of the worst kind? Is it homesickness or terror of vulgarity, and therefore snobbery? Look at those lamps in Bowery shops whose bases look like figures out of Versailles. Someone in Florence could be turning our Cambios into lamps and sending them back here, forgeries of forgeries." Pierra spoke in Italian and then switched to English. "We're a counterfeit reincarnation of Cambio."

"You've just figured this out?"

"What if Cambio was really a woman who posed as a man?"

"That's exactly what's going on." Claudia was exasperated. She left Pierra chipping off the rim of a halo and went down the street to do their laundry. When she returned Pierra was out. Claudia looked through her things. She looked in her drawers and in her closet, turning over shoe boxes and sticking her hands in pockets searching for a ticket back to Florence but found nothing.

FIGURES AND pictures were moved to one side so Claudia and Pierra could collapse exhausted in front of the television. They were too tired to do anything but sit in a cone of blue light with their feet resting on someone's head and a milk crate. They watched a program about a man who was to have a sex-change operation. He talked about how he felt trapped in the wrong body, and he had always felt that way. He had spoken to his girlfriend about it, but she didn't understand.

"I wouldn't either," Pierra said, "he's a nice-looking man." Dates traveled across the screen. "Don't do it," she said to the television.

"He feels he has to. It's not necessarily a simple choice."

The operations were gradual. There was plastic surgery, hormones, wearing women's clothing, trying to be a woman all the time.

"There's something wrong," explained a woman he worked with, "he's gone too far, too many bows and too much prancing. He doesn't have it right. Didn't he ever really watch women to see how we are? He has an idea of being a woman; it's the idea, not the experience itself."

"She's not very sympathetic," Claudia said. "Doesn't she know he's going to see this film?"

How much of a biological identity are you born with, how much is learned as you go along? asked a voice-over, as if it had an answer.

"You relearn an identity, as if you're a kind of character in a Cold War spy movie," Claudia said to the television in a flat voice.

Pierra changed the channel.

SHE DISAPPEARED a week later. Claudia searched among the package receipts, bills of lading, and envelopes fished out of the garbage but found no complete address for the dealer in Florence, only ends of street names and the word *Italia,* and that much she already knew. Her mother had the address of Pierra's family in Florence. Claudia wrote but never received a reply. That branch of the family, Claudia's mother only reconfirmed, had always been secretive and circumspect in an annoying way, as if they were always trying to put one over on you before you even knew what was up.

"Does she owe you any back rent? her mother asked over the phone.

"No."

"Good. I'm relieved," she said, as if whatever had happened had been Claudia's fault.

She tried to paint as Cambio, but she didn't know who he was anymore. Even an invented, assigned identity seemed a flimsy, immaterial thing floating past her, ungraspable and evasive. The view from her apartment was not one of red tiled roofs. The airshaft was not a courtyard; a sooty ailanthus wasn't some kind of olive tree. Cambio was dead. Pierra had murdered him, but the case against her was full of holes. She drew Pierra in the dock, but there was no judge or jury in the picture.

Gradually Claudia cleaned her apartment. For a few weeks paints and artificially aged drawing paper continued to arrive, but the room which had served as their studio was emptied out regardless. Claudia threw away jars of pigment, molds, caked brushes, swept away the last of the packing chips and marble dust, sold Pierra's C clamps, assorted vises, and chisels. She cleaned the crusted pigment from the white bowls and used them to drink coffee from. It had seemed naive to ask Pierra why she had wanted to fool people in the first place. Were the forgeries part of a scheme of revenge against the Florentine restorers? Was she a magnificent con artist for whom, even in her evasiveness, Italy and then New York became too hot? Had she objected to Cambio's cheap melodramas? Did she feel like the transsexual who would never get it right? Unasked questions no longer mattered to Claudia. She took apart what remained of the forgeries, hanging hats from plaster arms and what was left of the musical instruments.

SHE FOUND the journalists and other artists standing around in the corridor. One leaned out of a telephone booth and told a topical joke he'd just heard about a trial going on in Los Angeles. Someone told him it was a racist joke, and he should keep his voice down, but it wasn't clear if the person speaking was himself joking or offended. Claudia felt embarrassed by their bonhomie, which always left her out. As they waited they asked her where she'd been, but she'd no answer ready and was relieved when the conversation immediately took another turn. She almost fell asleep leaning against the wall until she was startled by the sound of someone calling a guard a pre-Cambrian idiot. The man was summoned downstairs to frisk people because the metal detector was on the blink, although how this was his fault no one knew. In her boredom Claudia twisted one of the loose buttons from a suit Pierra had left behind. The skirt was narrow, and she couldn't sit on the floor in it, but in a few minutes she finally gained admittance to a trial.

Unobtrusively taking a seat, she began to draw. It was the case of an artist who had printed money and plastered the bills all over the city, over buildings and signs, everywhere. He was a short, wiry young man who talked more than his lawyer would have liked. He claimed these were not counterfeits of fives, tens, or twenties, but real objects. He was too clever for his own good. Half the jury looked bored. Claudia was the only person really following his case. Why, the man testified, should there be a hierarchical relationship between the genuine currency and copies? Why is one more valuable than the other? He had no intention of passing out the bills he produced as actual money. The trial dragged on. Claudia finished her illustration, then went out into the hall. Only one television channel turned out to be interested in buying her drawings.

Later that day a murder trial began which was expected to have some publicity, and the crowd moved down the corridor toward it. A police informant had been shot and killed as she walked into a bodega. In a moment of accidental betrayal her cover had been blown by her partner, another informant. This trial was certain to be on the news, so Claudia abandoned the forger and followed the crowd toward a courtroom where there was actual money to be made drawing reenactments. The woman had left three children whose faces appeared on the front page of several newspapers, and so, following the shooting, undercover operations came under new scrutiny in the press and at city hall. As the surviving informant who would be called on to testify was led down the hall someone in the crowd pulled out a gun and threatened him. Claudia drew the man as fast as she could, his gun brandished in the direction of the informant. This would be worth money. He ran down the hall and although chased by guards he was swallowed up in the movement of people and never seen again. Perhaps Pierra had been right, impersonating a man concerned with the morphology of revenge was a waste of time. She no longer thought about the possibility of laughing all the way to the bank as she waited in the corridors where an obsession with evening the score, an attempt at retribution, generally reigned. As she listened to the testimony of the informant who blundered, and whose mistakes were fatal yet inevitable given the circumstances, she sharpened her pencils, let the shavings fall on the floor, and began to draw his likeness, penitent and nervous, a face which had no hope of shelter, he said, in this world or any other. She drew him leaning out a window watching the stabbing, helpless. In Claudia's picture, drawing what was imagined but not seen, blood spurted in fountains that defied gravity, just as in Cambio's melodramas. It was a fictitious setting, nineteenth-century and ridiculous, but she felt someone looking over her shoulder, laughing at what she had drawn although she hadn't intended to make a cartoon out of it.

The undercover policeman was a counterfeit man of the streets, and the counterfeit had failed. His true colors emerged in a split second of bad judgment, and the illusion of likeness faltered. Some detail or series of details, clothing or speech, gave the pair away. They didn't quite get it right.

In fact it wasn't the closeness of the resemblance that mattered, people are easily fooled, but whether you can stay in character. Pierra had fled, but with her departure the romantic Cambio took to his heels as well, rescinding offers of a life on beaches with singing palm trees. Overhead fluorescent lights buzzed, and Claudia, egged on by the banality of the familiar scene and the urgency of getting the job done in time, turned to the next blank page. She watched the man mime the scene of the murder until he stopped gesturing, then, one hand gripping the witness stand, he pointed at the accused gunman with the other. She drew him in that pose, then, as court was recessed, packed up her things to go home. After the pictures were sold they would be thrown away, useless, meaningless, case closed and forgotten.

The Cenci, her mother would say, nobody remembers them either and who cares anyway? They ran a restaurant on Tenth Avenue that made people sick. Be glad it shut down. In many ways she was.

Analogue

"Analogue" was written for the video *The In-Between,* by Carol Anne Klonarides and Michael Owen, as part of a series of pieces commissioned by the Wexner Art Center, designed by architect Peter Eisenman. The two stills printed here are reproduced courtesy MICA-TV © 1990.

I EXPECTED HER letters to be confessions. They lay in a thick pile next to my coffee. There was no one else in the room, cigarettes fell from a pack onto the floor, falling into a shape which resembled a stick man, and I said to him, You'll do as well as anyone: listen to this. You have to pay attention when somebody writes in this way with this kind of urgency. I read her impressions out loud to him. I used a skeptical tone of voice, exaggerated, supercilious, even speaking in different accents; sometimes lapsing into Inspector Clouseau French, sometimes a kind of Ian Fleming Russian, but I had the suspicion or at least indulged in the impression that my mute companion believed every word.

DEAR EDGAR,

Last night an incubus slept beside me. Had you been here you would have said I suffered from *un cauchemar* again, or pointing to the couch, you would say that narrow berth would give anyone bad dreams. You would tell me I was only afraid to fall off it, but this time I'm sure the incubus has stayed with me all day and will reappear at night. The incubus was a familiar woman, she looked a little like me and even a little like you, *une cauche-mère*. When I woke I

photographed the couch, pillows and blankets scattered all over. One hears of photographs of phantoms, they register on the film, even though you thought the camera was aimed at an empty space. Click. What you could have sworn was a bare corner, or just a ceiling, is revealed to contain, when the film comes back from the lab, a dusty shadow. You look closely at the picture, hold it up to your nose, someone slightly familiar grows apparent, but it's not yourself you see reflected in the pane. So I aimed the camera wherever there was available light, whether dead space or clutter. We'll see who turns up when the film comes back. I'll send you the pictures, even if nothing appears.

I've heard echoes of past parties, whispers of old arguments, the creakings of faltering, unfinished sentences, syllables boomeranging around as if caught in an echo chamber. I turn around quickly and try to catch her, but she is just half a second quicker than I am. I might see a shadow against a wall, and I'm sure the shadow isn't mine. I might see a foot hurry around a corner or a hand dangle from a ledge. What, I keep asking myself, what does this counterfeit want from me? One day I actually saw her standing in a tower, and I yelled up at her, but all I heard in response were echoes. I'm sure she's someone we know or have at least seen before.

Here's proof. Her presence reminds me of the following scene in *Duck Soup:* Chico Marx, while running from Groucho, shatters a mirror. Stepping into the space behind the glass he pretends to be Groucho's reflected self. Groucho hops. Chico hops. Groucho jigs. Chico jigs. There is a room behind the mirror, not a supporting wall, as is usually the case. Is the furnished space identical to the room in which Groucho cakewalks? If not, why doesn't Groucho appear to notice? Groucho drops his hat. Chico drops his hat. They change places. The gag continues in silence. For me the question remains: why was a mirror, frangible and deceptive, used to separate two rooms instead of plaster, sheetrock, and building studs?

Why am I explaining this to you? You never liked to spend much time here so I wouldn't be surprised if you don't really remember these rooms. The ceilings are probably higher than you give them credit for, and what you consider the representations of my personality—the combs, lipsticks, glasses, and ashtrays—don't loom as large as you think. The shoes and books on the floor you were sure were gunning for you when you tripped on them are still in place.

Yours,
Anne

DEAR ANNE, I wrote, let me tell you a story, a distraction. Once on a long train journey I began to talk to a woman who was sitting opposite me. It was night, but she was wearing a black hat with a veil drawn across it. She called herself Fac Totem, and she was running away.

I don't feel like myself, she said.

Who does?

She had worked as a cleaner for a woman who called herself Madame Sélavy. Sélavy spoke several languages, sometimes all at once. On her first day Sélavy told her to wait in *le couloir* while she dressed. Fac Totem thought she meant the cooler, and although she misunderstood, she was indeed in a kind of prison. Weeks passed, and as she swept and polished parts of Sélavy's house she couldn't find a door that led out of the building, and she sometimes thought she was fading into the house itself, she spent so much time touching its painted, tiled, mirrored, veneered, and stone-faced surfaces. Sélavy would often appear from behind a corner to check on her, or she would think she saw her in the distance, and so would try to clean with a little more energy. One night as she entered a back room which bracketed the structure like a parenthesis, she found a mannequin leaning against a staircase. It wasn't wearing any clothes; its face was featureless and painted over. She threw it on the floor.

One more thing to clean!

As she said those words, features began to color the dummy's face. It began to speak and at first she thought the voice came from a wall or column. She dressed the dummy in her clothes, and it took over her job, like a kind of golem. No one noticed the difference. The artificial worker labored harder than any human could, it worked so hard that Sélavy became exhausted just thinking up tasks, not realizing who was in fact executing her orders. Meanwhile, though half-naked having surrendered her clothes, Fac Totem was free to roam from room to room, looking, not cleaning. Stuck in a cornice she found a wedge of folded papers which she couldn't unfold, so tightly were they jammed together. The object seemed like something personal and organic, like a severed body part. She dropped it. In another room she discovered bicycle wheels, a bridal gown, and a bottle rack.

One night while holding the mannequin by the hand, they were discovered. When Sélavy saw the girl and her double she looked back and forth at the two of them, frantically searching for mirrors which she knew weren't in the room. She threatened the two with expulsion to a no-man's-land of urinals and constantly dripping taps. If Fac didn't pull the plug on her substitute there were going to be problems in the future.

Get rid of it.

The *sosie* pleaded with her. As Fac hesitated, Sélavy grabbed the double around the neck, and she crumbled to the floor in a heap. The girl was, naturally, forced to return to work. New cleaning tasks, twice as demanding as before, were assigned, so one night when she was sure the other woman was asleep, she stuffed her pockets with cash found behind a painting and ran away.

I was just a stranger on a train, but I asked if she would join me in the café car for a cup of coffee, thinking that was the least I could do, but she said, no thanks. She must have gotten off the train at the next station because I never saw her again.

Your shadows, doubles, and ghosts can take many forms.

Edgar

DEAR FAC T. FINDER,

Don't send me moral tales, please. Allegories can't explain the sightings I've described to you, as if these echoes could be reduced to a game a child might play while sitting in a waiting room. Fac Totem's story, as you told it, reminds me of *Find the Things* or *What's Wrong with This Picture?* Rrose Sélavy's chambers are now full of objects left behind by an exile: the Duchampian wedge, the nude descending the staircase, the *Bride Stripped Bare*. I found these things right off the bat, but felt no more victorious than if I had suddenly dropped a book which happened to fall open to a sought-after page.

Love,

Anne

INSIDE THE envelope were pictures of the house. It was a building I knew well, and all the pictures were empty. She imagined a girl on a tricycle pedaling down a long corridor as if being chased, but I found no afterimages, no configurations of light and shadow which could have been construed as a human figure. At least, I told my cigarette companion, that's how the pictures appeared at first glance.

I didn't write back for a long time, but her letters continued pursuing me, a shadow I couldn't detach.

DEAR EDGAR,

I'm afraid to leave the house. I wander around it for days.

If I go outside, this thing will follow me. If it walks out of a store without paying for a magazine or grabs someone's wallet, for example, I might be the one to be arrested, so I never open an outside door or lean out a window. As long as I can maintain my prison I'm safe, but this procedure has its drawbacks. I am getting sick of ordering pizza and Chinese food to be delivered to the side door. Sometimes I feel as if I'm running in circles, and my twin is right behind me, never catching up, never allowing me to turn around fast enough so that we collide. I saw her on a bridge that connects two halves of the building. I don't think you quite understand some of what I've been writing to you. The incubus isn't invisible, I can't wrap her in bandages, a kind of feminized Claude Rains, please, sometimes I don't think you're really listening. What is similar, and I'm sure of this, are bad intentions. As Claude Rains became the Invisible Man, he grew increasingly violent. Sometimes I'm afraid my incubus is corroding me, as bits of the house erode and others seem to appear. Perhaps I'm becoming part her and part myself. You wouldn't recognize the site as it looks now, half what it was, half what it might have become.

Sincerely and truly,
Anne

Dear Anne,

It's all right to see a woman on a bridge, but you're supposed to see a man on the tower.

Do you believe in the sentience of inert things? Maybe that's the problem. You think gypsum board and steel are going to turn and say, "Have a Nice Day!" or "Please come again!" Will marble tell you to keep your feet off its face and glass tell you to stop staring? The corners and windows take on personalities, but they aren't your friends. Are you turning everything around you into a massive memento mori? I don't have to walk those corridors, I can remember the sounds of footfalls down the passages. Benjamin felt he could read Baudelaire and never set foot in Paris. Enjoy your slice and pretend you're in Rome.

Best,
Edgar

IT WASN'T a very nice letter. I hoped it would at least make her angry at me and never write again. Somewhere in the distance I heard a recording of "I Put a Spell on You." I ignored the sound and began where I left off, prying the molding and wainscoting from a room on the ground floor. Crenellations on the exterior will be the next to go. Once they're off, I plan to paint in their shadows so there'll be a record of what used to occupy each space. I read that a fire broke out in one wing, and in those rooms I've erected model flames constructed from a heat-resistant plastic. Soon there may be no space remaining inside. For every removal, a residue is left over. The rate of accretion might eventually outweigh the removals, and I can imagine rooms in which no space remains.

DEAR EDGE GARE,

PRISONHOUSE
ROUGHHOUSE
NUTHOUSE → (SHIP OF FOOLS) → HOUSEBOAT
HOUSE ARREST
HOUSE SALAD   HAUSSMANN
HOUSEBREAK   HOUSE MUSIC
HALFWAY HOUSE   OUTHOUSE
JOHN HOUSEMAN   IN HOUSE
WAREHOUSE   OPEN HOUSE
HOUSEFLY   HOUSEBOUND
HOUSEBOY/MAID/MOTHER/DRESS FULL HOUSE
SAFE HOUSE   HOUSE OF MIRRORS

HOUSING	HOUSEBROKEN
HOUSEHOLD	HOUSE OF COMMONS
HOUSE OF CARDS	HOW'S EVERYTHING
HOUSE PARTY	ACID HOUSE
A. E. HOUSMAN	ANIMAL HOUSE
HOUSEKEEPER	PENTHOUSE
HOUSE OF THE RISING SUN	DOG HOUSE
FUNHOUSE	HOUSEPLANT

How is memory like a house which is constantly being constructed and torn down at the same time? What parts have been sandblasted away? Which pasted back together with Krazy Glue and Elmer's?

Yours,

Anne

THIS MORNING my companion was gone. I was sure I had left him on the table last night. I could remember turning his arms and legs as I read him Anne's last disturbing letter. You see something uncanny, and it may be nothing other than the familiar, briefly forgotten, then re-emerging in what seems to be another form. I could buy more cigarettes but didn't move. I searched the building all day, looking for anything small and white, like a figure, but not a person. In the evening I ordered out, Chinese food. The delivery boy arrived twenty minutes later. I asked him if he had seen anyone around the building. As he pocketed my change he told me that he had seen a man who looked just like me, and the man had waved to him from the tower. I told him that wasn't possible. I had been in the cellar for the past hour. The delivery boy was sure. The man who looked like me had waved and turned off a light. He assumed the man was descending to open the door. How can that be possible, I asked, there is no light in the tower. He shrugged, indicating that he had to be on his way, there were other deliveries. I gripped the bag of noodles and chicken in oyster sauce as if I were prepared to eat my words too, then asked if I could have one of his cigarettes. He gave me one, and I told him I would pay him for the rest of his pack if he would give it to me. In fact, I would pay double. I might not be able to get out for some time to come. He looked at me strangely, then handed me half a pack. I gave him several large bills folded into my back pocket. From the door I watched him ride away. Before he reached the street, he stopped his bicycle and turned to look upward, as if seeing a light on in the upper storeys of the building which I knew to be dim. I quickly leaned out the door to try to see what he might have been staring at, but the rest of the building was dark.

Hotel

Inside the hotel among the heterogeneous mob who for the most part had not dared to put their noses out of doors, a horrible atmosphere of suspicion had grown up. Various people were infected with spy mania and were creeping around whispering that everyone else was a spy of the Communists, or the Trotskyists, or the Anarchists or what-not.

—George Orwell, *Homage to Catalonia* (1937)

After a prodigious search I finally got someone to give me a rifle. I remember one day when I was with some friends on the Plaza de la Independencia and the shooting began. People were firing from rooftops, from windows, from behind parked cars. It was bedlam, and there I was, behind a tree with my rifle, not knowing where to fire. Why bother having a gun, I wondered, and rushed off to give it back.

—Luis Buñuel, "The Civil War,"
from *My Last Sigh* (1983)

WAITERS CIRCLED each table, brushing away nonexistent crumbs, repositioning plates and glasses, removing the lids of serving dishes as if there were something unexpected balanced on their arms. On bare china before each diner they placed two olives and a single cold sardine. There were no menus. These were stacked in the kitchen under tin vessels for dispensing olive oil whose bases left rings on them. In the kitchen the cook reached for one and tipped its thin spout over a two-handled iron pan, but nothing came out. There was nothing to put in the pan had there been any oil. He replaced the *setrill de llauna* on top of the papers and sat down to a glass of wine in an empty kitchen. Each diner will receive only half a glass of wine and no more. A shot pierced one of the windowpanes near the entrance to the hotel's dining room. Guests cut their individual sardines into slivers. No one paid attention to the sound. Later a waiter found the bullet while he was sweeping up. He put the slug in his pocket and fingered it as he walked home in the middle of the night.

TRUDE WAS pointed out to him as she left the dining room. She walked past his chair without noticing that he was watching her, pushing his glasses up his nose as she passed. Glancing at the hole the bullet had made in the glass and the surrounding cracks branching toward mullions like a spiderweb, she was careful not to step on shards or slivers. She had only one pair of shoes, and they were wearing thin. The man ran up to her as she began to climb the stairs to her room. He put a note in her hand written in simple, broken German.

A Spanish marriage with a nice man. All papers can be arranged. Price: 500,000 pesetas. Think about it. Will get in touch.

She turned around, but he had moved quickly toward the door and with a gravelly sound of heel against stone he was gone. She returned to the dining room and looked from one end of it to the other. Many remained at their tables poking olive pits around their plates, a man's eyes darted nervously toward another table, a woman looked at Trude in the doorway and smiled. Someone had told someone, someone had given her away.

In her coat pocket there was a transfer from a streetcar. It was torn in half, stamped with the word *strasse* and a few barely legible numbers. She thought she had a new name, convincing and beyond suspicion; the paper was the only clue to wherever it might have been that she came from.

HE HAD ARRIVED from the front lines near Huesca two days before they met. He described trying to walk with a rifle hidden under his clothes, the butt shoved under his armpit and the barrel running down his trouser leg. The bayonet couldn't be removed. He walked like the American comic Buster Keaton, or like a man who had been badly wounded, though in fact he was only a little scratched on his arms. If someone, thinking his awkward limp genuine, were to offer him a seat on a train or in a park, he would be unable to sit down. He would be discovered, but he had to travel and had no choice but to risk the trip. *There were hardly any guns,* he said, *and the one I found had to be hidden.* It was stolen from him one night when he had slept in an abandoned lunatic asylum, shattered and crumbling with barely a roof between uprights. She asked him how, if there was so little of the building left, he knew what it had been. There were bars on the windows, he said, and chains hung limply from the walls as if exhausted from an argument. But the most obvious signs of disturbed inmates were the drawings scratched on the walls. Monstrous faces, tongues, sexual organs with little arms and legs marched toward a crack in the wall. In the morning he got away as fast as he could. He had the kind of rifle used only by anarchists, he explained; anyone who found it would identify the gun as such and would come after him. He gave her a red scarf, and she tied it around her neck like a kind of tourniquet. Trude put her hand on his knee where the gun would have been and began to explain how she had arrived in the city, but they heard a shot fired from somewhere behind a ruin of a church and began to walk back to the hotel. As they walked she told him that she had thought once she crossed into Spain no one could send her back. It hadn't been easy getting in. Weeks before, in Toulouse, she discovered she hadn't the right papers. A man was found, a friend of a friend of a rumor, who would help her make the crossing on foot through the mountains.

"I met him in the basement of a printing house, sorting blocks of type with one hand. I spelled *b-o-r-d-e-r* along a line, and he, in turn, formed the letters of the place I was to meet him, then he dumped all the letters into a box. I left money by a typesetting case. He took the notes, counted them with blackened fingers. I almost didn't expect to see him again. Sometimes people who ask for payment in advance take all your money and disappear, or they turn you in, but he didn't. I don't know why. I don't know why he was any different."

He untied the red tourniquet, bound so tightly that his nails left marks on her neck.

"I heard women cost more. They climb slowly and draw attention."

"The climb wasn't that difficult." She tried to sound indifferent, although she knew she was unconvincing, even foolish, like an actor who ought to have been a comic but was caught in an American Western. She had to find another country. They compared their images of New York: towers of Babel on a floating island, a city of millions, each resident speaking one of a thousand languages. Men read lengths of ticker tape, and women drove cars. It might have been a mistake to have spoken to him about the trains, a one-armed smuggler, and a passport burned in Toulouse. He looked funny as he imitated how it looked to walk with a gun in one's pants, but the story of the drawings on the wall had the sound of invention. At night with no tallow, candles, or matches, how could he have seen them? When can a wall be more than a wall? When a gullible listener is found, a pile of stones becomes an asylum, a charnel house, an abattoir. He couldn't marry her. He was already married.

DETERMINED AND antsy, Katerina couldn't stop talking. She had a vague idea that she could be a pest, it was in her nervous system, but she also believed her instincts seldom deserved questioning. She recognized Trude by her accent when Trude asked if she could change her room. Katerina was standing by the front desk, overheard, and spoke for her, without pausing first to ask if she might be of help.

She was irksome in her jacket with big pointed lapels, this strange woman who intervened, a woman who seemed to guess immediately who Trude was and what she wanted, a woman who climbed over people, not mountains. Trude had tried to be diplomatic, even apologetic when she complained about the noise that came from the family living in the rooms upstairs. *I understand this may be difficult to change. . . .* Katerina elbowed in, emphatic with the clerk at the desk, she wouldn't take no for an answer. Her tone was condescending, almost insulting, and Trude edged away from her in embarrassment. The day manager ignored her. The days when he had to bow before this kind of treatment by guests were over, but Katerina's ire over Trude's sleepless nights indicated that his dignity meant nothing to her. *Just do as I say.*

Trude looked toward the door, whispering, *But I don't know you at all.* Katerina, sure of her authority and sure of the validity of her demands, appeared deaf. In a few minutes Trude would have to thank the stranger, and she decided to do so in Spanish. When the negotiations were over and the day manager went back to his paper, Katerina took Trude's arm and steered her away from the desk, out of earshot. Her hair was colored blonde, but the darker strands close to her parting were moving downward because bleach or dye was impossible to find in the city.

In her room at night they whispered in German, lying on Katerina's bed because there were no chairs. They discovered that they both knew a man from Berlin who had departed from Heidelberg intending to travel to Amsterdam. He claimed he would make it to New York, but Katerina thought he'd never get that far. Trude agreed. He'd stop when he sighted any significant body of water. She found herself speaking quickly, nervously, unconsciously parroting Katerina's cataract of words. *Short man with one arm living in a printer's basement.* Trude spoke first, then Katerina agreed with her. Without understanding why she abandoned her reserve, Trude felt her tone of voice turn demanding, exasperated and shrill, just like Katerina's, even when she remembered out loud, only recollecting names that had to be changed and Gothic spires in the snow.

Katerina had come very close to acquiring Spanish papers. She found a man who wanted her to pretend to be his wife. The ruse wasn't difficult, they had rooms directly next door to one another, rumored to be adjoining, but no connecting door actually existed. A few hours after dinner Katerina would go to his room, but when she arrived he would sit with his back practically in her face and write at an uneven table which functioned as a desk. The pool of light from a small lamp left part of his head in shadow. He had a peaked crown and receding hairline so that the illusion he unwittingly presented each night was one of a man in a kind of dunce's cap; although industrious and silent, he was no dummy. She asked him what he wrote, but the answer, *accounts,* seemed a false floor to her. Writing, for Katerina, had to be about words, letters, narrative perhaps, but as she watched his hand travel across page after page, even from across the room, she could have predicted that his gestures weren't those of someone making the short jerky strokes required for adding columns of numbers. He had to be writing phrases and sentences, but she was afraid that if she got up and looked over his shoulder he'd slam the ledger in her face. Despite her anxiety that she'd go blind in the dim light, she still brought a book with her; there was nothing to do otherwise but watch bugs crawl up the wall until she fell asleep in a chair. Days went by, but the arrangement continued to be purely for show, and Katerina tried not to grow impatient. Too much depended on appearances. Just when she felt at the end of her rope from being shunned and ignored, from being treated as inanimate as a paperweight that only snowed if shook, he seemed to sense he had gone too far. Taking her arm, he would sit with her at dinner and breakfast. He spoke to her, if not with affection, then with a certain familiarity, which to an observer might seem genuine. He knew she took her coffee black and never offered milk or sugar. These gestures of familiarity might calm her for an hour. If residents of the hotel found her pushy, she needed signs that indicated she was not so. She wasn't marooned, an orphan, an oddball, a non sequitur, an entry in an accounting book.

If police passed her in the street she was sure it was only a matter of time before she betrayed herself, and betrayal could take several forms. Blurting out an obscene phrase as they passed, or spilling something on their uniforms; she could do these things involuntarily like a robot, like a doppelgänger, a similar version of herself, but not herself exactly, one who would think, *Might as well jump off the cliff, since I'm going to fall anyway.* Katerina, awake in a stranger's room at night, could imagine these scenes with what seemed to her to be alarming veracity. She had heard him refer to her as the woman he was going to marry, and even on one occasion as his wife, but whenever she asked about the papers she had been promised, he would say only that she would get them soon, maybe even tomorrow. She couldn't wait. She tried to do whatever was demanded of her, but felt she was suffocating in the uncertainty his delay induced. Even while suspecting she'd never get anything from him, Katerina kept the ruse going out of habit and frustration. Bored watching bugs on the wall and ruining her eyes, feeling ridiculous, but at the same time like a prisoner, she slipped out of his room one night only to bump into a man with a broken leg. Katerina struck a match against a wall to see more clearly. Light bounced off the skeleton frame of a crutch as he hurried away the best he could, as if anxious to save face; little did he know the whole pretence had been for nothing.

The following day Katerina made out the figure of her ghost husband walking down a street. He had stopped in front of a shop in order to look through maps and a few books offered for sale on a table outside. Police were walking toward her, and in a panic she crossed the street; running up to the table she put her arms around him, greeting him before he could speak.

Have you lost your mind? The writer of fictitious accounts pushed her away. No one else was on the street, no one looked out the windows; the police, as they marched, didn't seem to notice either of them. In the violence of his shove a few unfolded maps fluttered to the sidewalk. Pinar del Río, Nueva Gerona, Havana were points on the pavement, then blew away. Katerina looked down on a cartography of pavement cracks. He walked past her as if she were invisible.

Rather than chase after him or grab his arm, Katerina walked in the opposite direction. To say he was being a snob wasn't accurate; the word *snob* belonged to former social situations, and when it came to a show of cold shoulder, she could out-snub anyone. The frustrated embrace on the street signified betrayal and marked the end of their arrangement. At the hotel he would no longer speak to her. She told Trude that the truth was she hadn't enough money to pay what he demanded.

TRUDE DIDN'T like to leave the hotel, but Katerina couldn't bear the dark rooms any longer than was absolutely necessary. In a corridor, under the slow clock, she would greet Trude as if she were a long lost comrade and insist they look around the city they'd come so far to hide in. Before going out, Katerina engaged in a ritual of polishing their shoes, although polishing meant only rubbing cracked leather with the end of a sheet. The operation was too feeble to actually shine their shoes. Dirt fell off. That was all. Blonde hair disappearing, she pulled her veil over her face, tucked Trude's red scarf under her collar, and marched her into daylight, steering her by the elbow as if she were the navigator of a faltering ship. Despite being in charge and able to speak better Spanish, Katerina felt she might blurt out any words that entered her head at any moment, thereby endangering them both for no reason other than a breakdown of control, a sudden, inexplicable loss of nerve. Ironically Trude looked slightly Spanish, but Katerina, who spoke so well and so freely, did not. *We make,* Katerina said, *a pair of Siamese twins. You look the part, and I do the talking.*

Toward evening they heard firing, sometimes in the distance, sometimes nearby. Once Trude observed a man sitting in a park reading a newspaper while a series of shots rang quite close. They ran behind a wall, but he remained oblivious. Perhaps, Katerina said, he's deaf, but Trude thought his oblivion was one not of deafness but of resignation. She remembered seeing his head turn when a dog barked on the other side of the plaza. It began to rain, and he finally hurried away with the pages covering his head, like a cartoon character who might notice the bullet holes in his papers only when rain fell through them.

"CALL ME foolish," Dr. Van de Lune began. No one nodded. Katerina's attention wandered. She looked around the dining room, but the accountant hadn't come down. The Dutchman explained that he had located a very old and rare diamond necklace, a discovery that marked the culmination of a decade's long search, and although he couldn't buy the whole strand himself, he was now looking for investors to aid him in his plan. Once arduously traced, the diamonds turned out to belong to an ignoramus who would probably settle for a price that would represent a fraction of their real worth, allowing the investors to resell at a large profit. He wiped his glasses in appreciation of his own invisible efforts. Trude asked him about obstacles presented by the war, random shelling, bombs, buildings collapsing, but he explained that since the necklace was here in Spain he had no choice. He had chased a queen's diamonds all over Europe and happily landed in this spot. He gestured around the table as if it were the best place in the world to be.

This may explain the appearance of the well-dressed men who call on Dr. Luna, thought a waiter who eavesdropped on the table. His visitors were show-offs in the city where one rarely saw such displays of privilege.

"*Quelle reina?*" A small man with an Italian accent joined the group. He had arrived at the hotel the previous night. He was very tired from days of traveling and wasn't sure what language he ought to speak.

"Marie Antoinette," Dr. Van de Lune said. Then he looked at the waiter and added "*putain autrichienne*" as if to prove where his sympathies lay. The waiter understood one of the two French words, and smiled. Van de Lune looked at the Italian for a flicker of intelligent familiarity. "Revolution," he said, making circular motions as if stirring a great vat with both arms. His elbow jabbed a man to his left who introduced himself as Jack Twig.

Jack had spent the previous month at the front, his left leg was stiff and lay straight on a chair in front of him. He smelled a rat in Van de Lune, suspecting the Dutchman would probably collect money from the investors and run. Van de Lune patted his good leg with a familiarity that annoyed Jack, but he was unable to move without commotion and fanfare so he stayed put. The Dutchman continued to talk about the history of the necklace.

Katerina looked toward the stairs for the keeper of accounts. After the encounter in the hall, she had watched Twig arrive with one small bag. He had tipped his hat and limped past. She thought he was freckled, ugly, and of no use whatsoever. No one, she told Trude, ever arrived at the hotel with lapdogs, servants, and more bags than she could count. It was a disappointment.

Van de Lune stared at Trude, and she looked away. Everyone, she felt, knew that she was desperate, and to a man like the doctor, who appeared oblivious to the fighting and, as a result, knew little of what was going on in the city, her search for a husband was of only lascivious interest, unmitigated by the reasons for it.

Putain autrichienne, Van de Lune repeated, and he winked at Jack.

In the silence that followed the doctor's story the Italian fell asleep, having only vaguely grasped syllables in three languages and unable to speak. Jack too felt sleepy. He wondered again why the story was being told to strangers. The diamonds might have been a smoke screen. The woman he'd seen in the hall at night smiled stiffly at him, without turning red at all, not even pink, while her friend looked on in agony when Van de Lune used the words *une orgiaste* in connection with the necklace. No longer paying attention to the sound of the doctor's voice, he tapped his fingers on the table while staring aimlessly at the woman sitting across from him. Van de Lune felt he was in a room filled with riotous children and gave up attempting to signal chumminess to them. He had only been humoring these people. They didn't know it. Their peril was none of his concern. Go ahead, he thought the Englishman was saying, I'm bored so make me nervous.

"Catalonia is a long way from Versailles." Twig rose with his stiff leg dead to the world, said good night to everyone at the table, and pivoted around on his crutches. The Italian helped him upstairs.

COOK TOLD the waiter there were no diamonds in Barcelona, only spies who pretended to look for them while actually hunting for something else. Well-dressed visitors who called on the doctor were decoys, hiding motives completely unrelated to a headless French queen. He wants to make you think one thing when something else, something quite different, is really going on, the cook explained very slowly. Doctor Luna wouldn't speak so freely about diamonds the size of starling eggs and he wouldn't dress like an empty-handed baker's assistant if he didn't expect to be followed and robbed. A con artist, the cook said, and went back to his empty pots.

LOURIA KNEW Katerina went to Cordoba's room at night, but he also knew she did absolutely nothing when she was there apart from sitting in a chair for a few hours. He had changed his name from Levi, and was considering changing it again. *Lorrechia,* he said out loud. *Lapin. Lampedusa. Leopardi.* He had no identity cards. He could be anybody. On the boat from Naples he watched the cabin boy—legs of his trousers dirty white, sliver of back showing above them—lean over the deck and stare at the sea. *What is the object of desire of my object of desire?* he whispered to himself. He was to have gotten off the boat at Corsica but decided he would go as far west as he could. The rest of the crossing was calm. He kept away from other Italians, the French, and Spaniards on the boat, but he did learn that the cabin boy had jumped ship in Corsica and had been replaced by a Moroccan, not young, who looked angrily at Europeans who came on deck when he was there.

His hotel room contained two mirrors, one whole, the other de-silvered around the edges, and he spent an hour before dinner looking into them, checking his teeth and combing the hair on the back of his head. He hadn't taken much with him, but he had brought two possessions which suggested his life in Rome: a white shirt and a tortoiseshell cigarette case that had belonged to his mother. In the evening he tried to sit at Cordoba's table, although there was no food or wine to linger over. He nudged Louria's foot while Katerina smashed a sardine head with her knife. At night Cordoba knocked on his door. They spoke briefly. *Levi. Louria,* he whispered. He wondered how Cordoba knew his real name and offered him a cigarette, bought in Corsica and saved, since tobacco, he knew, would be scarce in Spain. Cordoba reached for him, and as he began to return the embrace, they stepped backward into his room, shutting the door without looking down the hall. Later Louria wondered if he had heard the clumping of the English Jack or the heels of one of the women at a far end of the corridor. It was night but not very late when Cordoba left for his room, and Louria went for a walk in the city. He walked past a dismantled church, thinking about how transgression went hand in hand with desire, and how he always wanted those things fenced in by markers of transgression. A woman carrying candles in a mitered hat held upside down brushed by him, without apologizing or excusing her touch or her stolen bucket. She was followed by a child holding two lit candles that appeared to have been gouged from their holders in one of the chapels; both rushed past him as if he were invisible. He wouldn't stroll that way again. Better to walk past a bank or a salumeria.

Cordoba came again the second night but left quickly, saying he was expecting a visitor. Louria didn't know if he should tell him that he knew about Katerina. He had seen her knock on his door and he waited, leaning against the wall, smoking, surprised she didn't notice the lit end of his cigarette bouncing in the dark. When his feet grew tired he perched on a table for nearly an hour, but Katerina didn't come out again. Without being told, Louria understood they had an arrangement about papers. Feeling relieved he went back to his room. He himself had been advised to strike a similar deal when a Spanish woman approached him on the boat, but he'd suspected she was really some kind of prostitute or extortionist and avoided her.

The third night he thought he heard Cordoba whisper *It's me,* but when he stepped into the hall someone struck him, from behind or front, in the dark he couldn't be certain. When he came to there was blood on his white shirt and his cigarette case was cracked into many pieces. He limped downstairs. The manager told him the accountant had disappeared without paying his bill. Louria avoided Katerina who also looked shaken and sat in a corner with her friend. The man with the bad leg said Cordoba always had cigarettes. Franco controlled the Canary Islands where tobacco was grown and whoever smoked Spanish cigarettes could be viewed with suspicion. Katerina pulled her veil down and batted an olive around her plate with a tineless fork. Trude stared at the broken window. Louria went upstairs, put the fragments of tortoiseshell in his pockets, and sat with the door open, waiting for men in uniform whom he imagined loaded down with cigarettes from the Canary Islands, smoking several at a time and speaking in Castilian.

THE POLICE stopped her in front of the Cinerama. They asked her name, and she said she was only going into the movies, carefully pronouncing *I'm going in here,* as if that were her name. She pointed to a poster although she hadn't read what was printed on it. She knew the drawing was of two women who looked at each other from a distorted perspective. A man's head, greatly enlarged, lay in the space between them, black hair, a mustache, and behind the image of his head Katerina thought she had glimpsed an Eiffel Tower that would signify the movie took place in Paris, but in the instant they asked for her name again it occurred to her that the long gray spire might have been the Tower of Pisa, so she didn't say she was going to see a French movie. She just said her name.

Two men took her elbows, just as in the movies. She didn't struggle, but she had an image of how she might look from behind, being taken by the arms like a kind of moving sandwich. She hoped no one she knew would see her, but the impulse to avoid embarrassment was vestigial, left over from her old life when running into people at the wrong moment meant only that you wanted to be alone or didn't want to be seen doing whatever it was you were doing. *Being seen with. Caught going into.* There wouldn't be anyone to carry tales about her, she wasn't rounding a corner in Berlin, and the future held nothing but embarrassment and humiliation only if she was lucky. They put her in a car and drove her to the other side of the city to a former office building whose cellar, more like a pit beneath the foundation, held men and women thrown in together. No one spoke to her, but it was clear some had been there for days or longer. Men and women lay in heaps as if sleeping in the middle of the afternoon. After an hour her name was called and she was taken upstairs to a large room on the second floor.

Men occupied every part of the room, busy with papers or talking among themselves. Some of the windows had been knocked out. No one had replaced the glass. A torn map of the city had been nailed to a wall beside her chair, and by twisting around to look at it she could see red and black marks, circles and crosses scattered over the streets and squares, but she didn't know what they meant.

When a man kicked her leg she claimed to be from Navarre. The police didn't believe her. He explained there was one way she could save herself. She could name others. He offered her a cigarette, and she took it. No one would know the information came from her, and she would be assured safety. A fly buzzed around the brim of her interrogator's hat, and she watched it as if hypnotized by its frantic hovering in the smoke. There were sinkholes everywhere, and she was sick of it. *If you're going to fall you might as well jump.* They promised her she would be rewarded for jumping, they already knew what was what anyway. She told them she didn't know anybody, but they had her address and knew she must have spoken to other hotel residents once in a while. They assured her they already knew who was who. It was only up to her. She could only hope to save one person.

TRUDE TRIED to find the man who had mimicked a stroll with a gun down his leg. As she sat waiting at the Plaza de Cataluna, she thought all the men around her looked like El Greco figures but without any dome of angels between their heads and the sky. Years ago she had seen El Greco's portrait of Cardinal de Guevara, the Inquisitor of Seville; his eyes were magnified by thick black glasses, and he grasped one chair arm tightly while the other hand dangled. It had been a frightening portrait even without the title, even without knowing who he had been and what he did, but the painting had been bought by a woman who lived in New York. The canvas cardinal was safe. Trude noticed people standing in doorways and wondered if a sniper had been seen on a rooftop. If shooting was about to begin she knew she should leave, but she continued to wait because she couldn't be certain firing would begin, and she needed to speak to the man who had walked with an imaginary gun down his leg. Sometimes they only wanted to shoot at the Christs and figures of Mary, executing them, and laughing on the way home. She would laugh too.

She pushed dirt around with the tip of her shoe, drawing vague characters from memory, then wiping them out. Goya's *Custody of a Prisoner Does Not Require Torture:* brown wash, man bent as if shackled in a room with a low ceiling. *Lunatic Freed Because He Erred* looked like a man asleep. She'd studied them in a book as if they'd been warnings, but at the time she'd been sure the warnings had nothing to do with her. She had looked at them and imagined claustrophobia but not really terror. Shooting began from a nearby apartment building, and she finally ran away down a side street. When she returned to the hotel a note had been left for her at the desk. He had disappeared, arrested, held in jail, no one knew on what charges or if he was still alive.

DR. VAN DE LUNE said, "I know something about betrayal, I've seen letters from prison, from those waiting for the guillotine, turned in by friends. I've seen agonizing documents written to family and accusers at the eleventh hour." He had translations in his room that he would be happy to show her. Why, if they existed at all, had he brought these documents with him? Why pack your only bag with letters sent during the Terror? He took Trude's arm, and his voice changed. Suddenly he was squatting in a Berlin alley, making a deal with someone he thought he could fleece. *See, lots of people get into the same jam. You're not alone.* He had never been betrayed by a confidant because he had no friends. His usually formal language seemed to have abandoned him, and he clung onto platitudes as if they were the only pegs that stuck out from walls as he made his descent. She wasn't sure if he had been waiting for her or if their meeting was a coincidence. Van de Lune drew her into a corner of the hall. Trude took a step away from him, but he clutched her elbow and pulled her closer. Katerina had called him the Diamond King. It had been a joke between them: the Diamond King, here comes the Diamond King. *With the millions coming to him, he could get us out of here. Why don't you marry him, then? Are you kidding? Why don't you?*

Trude thanked him for his concern, but he wouldn't let go of her arm. He scoffed at the words *thank you.* His eyes were red and wet. He wanted to know why she avoided him, everyone seemed to, wherever he went, and he wanted to know why. He was convinced she knew the answer. She would know why even those he'd never met avoided his overtures of interest and in fact seemed to hate him on sight. He was left out of everything. *I'm sure that's not true. What about your investors?* At her reminder, he changed his tone, and although still pleading, offered to share the diamonds with her. He cornered Trude so that she couldn't say no without joining the unknown group that always said no.

"I couldn't really, but it's very nice of you." She thought she sounded English and disarming, not like herself.

He began to scream at her. There were no diamonds, it was just a trick to get into Spain and to remain in Catalonia without drawing the kind of suspicion which would lead to his deportation. He put his face very close to hers. She yanked out of his grasp, ran downstairs and out into the street.

There are no diamonds! There was no Marie Antoinette!

Jack was on the sidewalk poking a fallen sign with one end of his crutch. Looking back through the glass Trude imagined she saw the Dutchman walking sadly under the hotel clock, glancing her way as if he intended to apologize, which would only make her feel more burdened. "Oh, tell." She thought Twig addressed her in English. He was cheerful and asked if she'd give him a hand. If she gave Twig a hand this one time he might turn into a kind of Diamond King and not ever let her go. She didn't want to speak to Jack I'll-Save-the-World either. She ran on. Trude realized only later Twig had been reading aloud the sign that had fallen to the street, *hotel.*

WHY DID HE know so much about France? What about Vermeer, tulips, and The Hague? Perhaps he's not who he appears; he's Dr. Lunette from Bordeaux, Dr. Window from Brighton. He's Dr. Lunatic.

She was on the train back to Berlin. Once she was in France, she forgot about the days before her deportation. Coffee after coffee made her delirious, her thoughts leaped from one fantastic tangent to the next, and their trajectory would draw a shape like a constellation whose final form and location were really just a guess. She imagined a scenario that would take place when she returned in which things would prove not to be so bad. They had been alarmists to think of leaving. Everyone who left would return within a few months, and everything would be as it had been a few years ago. They would laugh when she told them she had seen blood on the streets, and hair, and fragments of bodies, until she herself would stop believing she had ever seen these things. When Katerina returned, Trude would pass her on the boulevards as if she didn't exist, and she would get some satisfaction from high-hatting her. She threw the crumpled streetcar ticket out the window.

THE DINING ROOM was nearly empty. Fewer guests meant perhaps two sardines per diner and more chunks of bread that tasted of plaster. As near as the sea was, nothing seemed to come out of it, and the cook dreamed of fishermen's romesco contests where tomatoes and almonds were grilled together, and he shook pans as if they contained fish poached in golden wine and aromatic herbs. A waiter juggled oranges which had suddenly arrived by the truckload. The surfeit of oranges would rot beside shelves lined with empty oil tins and glass-stoppered jars. The waiter had begun a collection of spent slugs arranged around a terra-cotta floor tile. The bullets looked like metal roaches that came out at night in search of crumbs or smears of olive oil. As if they were real everyone was careful not to kick them. The dining room was quiet, the waiter was bored, thinking of his collection, and realizing that the kinds of traces which only had meaning to an insect were all that were left reasonably intact and alone.

Incunabula #1

In 1789 THE number of Frenchmen who could sign their name was one in two. The number of women who could sign their name was one in four. So someone else signed for you. One party was hired to commit forgery, but the substitution was considered entirely legitimate. Since over half the population required signatory stand-ins, some grew rich in service of the illiterate. The signers could act as doubles, could represent without bearing responsibility for the consequences of what was being signed. It was, for the stand-ins, a kind of ready-made disappearing act.

DURING THE early part of the next century, more citizens became capable of signing their names, but only those who could pay eighty francs a year for subscriptions read newspapers. The average worker in Paris, according to records kept by government and private agencies, earned less than eighty francs a month, so this part of the population relied more on what they heard rather than what they read by chance. Information, after a certain number of repetitions, might grow increasingly distorted, but bits of paper found lying around in the street didn't always contain the whole story either. Rumor and half truths, hearsay and gossip gained tremendous currency. There was no other choice. Historians later wondered if this meant that one class lived in a blur of mistakes, while members of another conducted their lives in an atmosphere of accurate judgments and predictability. (The dilemma of the historians reflects their trust in print.)

Written civilization was held hostage by the near uniqueness and expense of all printed matter. Frozen in the ambiguous status of semiprecious object, books didn't circulate
and were often displayed but not read by their owners. Most
thieves couldn't read and thought books useless rather than
objects of rarity and value. Printed matter, obscure and difficult to identify, was the safest sign of wealth, and therefore
relatively immune from theft. There are records of affluent
people who turned their cash, jewelry, gold, lottery tickets,
and paintings into vast libraries. Unknowing robbers who
broke into these rooms turned away in disgust.

When the practice of printing books was transformed
from small-time guild operations into businesses engaged
in mass production, what had once been rare and available
to only a few became something ordinary and taken for
granted. Eventually, almost anyone could break into the
territory of written civilization. Citizens didn't have to own
a castle in order to own a book. Thieves still closed the door
on libraries in disappointment. It wasn't just that books
became less castlelike in expense, but also in meaning. Less
remote, more accessible: if citizens hoped to affect a kind of
social advancement through literacy, they had to know what
to read. In other words, to think of literacy as a way of im-
proving your lot could be a mistake. Those books/avenues
didn't necessarily lead anywhere. One would not, for example, get far reading the kind of cheap novels described
as industrial fiction. The audience for such writing was referred to as vulgar readers, and it was felt that they threatened to swamp the marketplace with their desire for pulp,
pornography, and general gossip.

As literacy and print production increased, two kinds of
reading developed: narrative and nonnarrative. Reading
books was one thing; reading leases, loan agreements, maps,
catalogues, almanacs, and letters another. For a long time

one rarely mixed with the other. Narrativity was considered the mark of feminine interests, and its absence signified the presence of more masculine pursuits.

An inventive strategy for selling books was the introduction of the serial. Episodic fiction popularized print. Readers wanted to know what happened next. . . .

Year	*Number of titles published in France*
1789	2,000
1889	15,000
1914	25,000

THE ANARCHISTS wrote for each other. They didn't involve themselves in the mass production of texts, nor did they engage in the tricks of procuring a large audience. They were excluded from legitimate publishing and so operated on their own small scale.

IT BEGAN when a prefect of the police in the eleventh arrondissement needed a dependable source of information. Anonymously, through a series of mediators, he solicited writers and a printer and duped them into founding an anarchist magazine. Copies were delivered to the prefecture and the anarchists' meetings were recorded. The magazine was so successful, many imitators were encouraged to try to duplicate it. The prefect's office soon became filled with incriminating journals, newspapers, diaries, and apocrypha. Computer-coded copying machines were installed, and corridors became lined with file cabinets. Each morning the prefecture would be crowded with imitation anarchists, twins (identical and fraternal), photographers and their assistants, homunculi, actors, tearjerkers, iconoclasts, duplicates, replicates, twins of twins. Along the walls were stacked photocopies of photocopies going back hundreds of generations, and even the last blurred copy was filed somewhere. Wings had to be added to the prefecture, and extensions added to the wings. New archives were built. Card catalogues were put on microfilm. More personnel were hired: the duplicitous and the genuine. There were distinctions between the two, but the distinctions were often contradictory. The director of the bureau of internal plagiarism resigned, and his office was converted into headquarters for the repairmen of the photocopying machines, now on permanent staff. They soon developed their own archival system. The archives contained fragments mutilated by the machines but upon whose forgotten usefulness the repairmen thought a promotion might hinge, and so these were saved.

Incunabula #2

TRACY GOT A JOB in the basement during the Christmas rush. She reported to the front desk but was sent to a small office adjoining a stockroom. Even though the museum upstairs was now very busy, she was often idle, and so had the opportunity to waste a lot of time between processing orders for nativity cards and model pyramids. She unpacked crates labeled DO NOT OPEN, removing heavy, expensive catalogues to find images of fin de siècle Berlin or Russian Constructivist abstractions wrapped around uncracked bindings. She unwrapped warped remaindered books with coppery dust jackets, lives of Victorian self-mythologists in multiple volumes, autobiographies of Dadaist architects. In rooms formed from carton stacks she read short histories of medieval France where, due to the rarity of mirrors, many citizens never knew what they looked like, relying instead on the observations of others, and Renaissance Italy where heretics threw books against walls of the papal city, futile gestures which only doomed them. She unfolded maps and color reproductions that fell to the floor like accordions, but as Pandora's boxes they were disappointing. Trying to stay out of the airless office as much as she could, she occasionally heard her name called in the distance, but generally she calculated her reading time for spells when she wouldn't be missed. She cut out sections of books and tacked them above her desk. No one seemed to notice when the defaced books were sent upstairs to the museum gift shop.

Margaret of Navarre was a patron saint of Andrea del Sarto, Leonardo da Vinci, and Benvenuto Cellini, a constant liar. While her brother, Francis I, was king of France, ships were sent to Canada under the command of Jacques Cartier. Margaret tried to persuade Francis to sail with him so that he might assure himself of the kingdom of Canada, to confirm that it existed and that it was truly his. The British claimed to have already been there, but the descriptions of all that ice and acres of fir trees had the ring of something Cartier, like Cellini, might have invented to mask the reality of a tropical continent with cities of gold. The object of her scheme was to get rid of her brother, but the king suspected her motives and would not relinquish France to his sister. She was happy during his occasional departures. The absence of his criticism meant that she would not be made to feel as if she were constantly saying the wrong thing. Francis often made her pay for her apparent lack of forethought, and she was sick of being made to feel stupid.

Margaret and her court dined on rice for the first time. It was brought from the East and, not knowing how it was eaten in China, they boiled the grains with honey and fruit. Francis wasn't satisfied with being a lowly importer; he wanted direct access to Asian ports. Margaret thought he was being a pig and hoped he would disappear in the Adriatic. From her window, she saw flat-bottomed boats laden with guns and cannon made in Navarre. In 1544, her brother fought Charles V of Spain over the kingdom of Naples. Francis lost, and they rarely ate rice afterwards. Although he returned alive, the battle over Naples left Francis in a state of humiliation and impoverishment. Now you're the bore, she told him, and everyone knows it.

The museum basement, windowless and honeycombed with offices and storage facilities, bore no resemblance to a castle but might have been looked at as a kind of fortress. Tracy had a brother who got on her nerves occasionally, but the closest he came to being a king was when he had a summer job as the Prince in the Snow White section of Storytown in Lake George. Although working as the Prince, he had his eye on Peter Pan, and Tracy knew they met behind a wall on Captain Hook's island where no one could see them.

SHE SHOULD have filed order forms as soon as they were sent down by clerks in the museum gift shop upstairs, but as a rule she left them out on her desk for days until they formed a small stack. Thinking it would be more efficient if she did them all at once rather than one at a time, a piddling although indisputably more expedient technique, she accumulated all kinds of forms. If the manager planned a visit to the stockroom she would file them all at once. Otherwise she saw no point in it. The manager, when he realized she had little to do, threatened to assign her other tasks. For example, delicate pieces, the museum's reproductions, often were delivered wrapped in newspaper which had to be removed, then the copies of gold-plated Mexican ornaments or mechanical animals had to be rewrapped in tissue paper. It was not really part of her job but she unpacked a few of the objects and read the crumpled papers. Newsprint came off on her hands. She read the print straight across columns, ignoring dividing lines.

"To support the terrorist policy of   Searching for all-consuming passion . . . the American leaders," Mr. Ortega   Dare not abandon hope. Tous les Caleçons said, "allies and agents of imperialism   answers love's reckless cry. Jacket $90 who act from some political parties,   ribbed turtleneck, $72, and skirt, $34 press outlets or religious institutions   wool. Cotton crew-necks, $32 and leggings
  Government officials say it is no   Visit our new Tous les Caleçons shop in coincidence that political opposition   Expressions on the 3rd fl, Herald Square has become more strident at the same   And on Saturday, Oct. 19 meet designer time as rebel forces are preparing new   Gilles Charriot, from noon to 2 P.M.

SHE USUALLY brought her lunch with her and ate it in the basement. She didn't like going out because the restaurants near the museum were expensive and crowded, the walks in the park freezing cold, and the park itself was barren. Lit by blinking and buzzing fluorescent tubes, the basement was cool and smelled of rat traps. Somewhere in its recesses a radio could be heard. Occasionally one of the stockboys would enter the office, lend her his Walkman or bring her a Coke from upstairs. They called this working through lunch and reported it as overtime. The stockboy explained to her how simple it was to steal minor books and reproductions if inventory was sloppy and reports done in pencil. The basement was vast, there might be suits of armor, fur coats and crates of Cadillacs hidden in it. You could drive one away and no one would be able to tell it was missing. He was working on a system to fence some of the gold reproductions and jewelry. For the books he couldn't get much. Caravaggio, he said, who cares?

When the stockboy went to the circus he brought back for her a small blue bear which had been part of a prize. He had seen Helmut Holiday, the Human Cannonball, who wore flesh-colored tights with gold sequins around his hips, and as he hurtled above the ring he looked like a Christmas ornament before it shatters. The stockboy was a little slow and had found pleasure in endless but simple conjectures. He talked about the possibility of the Human Cannonball losing his flimsy costume, sequins falling all over the place, and about his own fear of doing anything headfirst. Most importantly he had been unable to resist the freaks. The freaks, he said, were outstanding. The Anatomical Man was some kind of contortionist who sucked in his stomach until you could see the spools of his spine while he simultaneously stretched out his neck. Fish Girl was covered in a slimy skin and glared at him from her tank. Otis the Frog Boy was also disgusting. A woman called the Queen of the Tigers had real fur and sat in a cage with a mangy tiger. He knew the freaks were all fakes, but he didn't grow bored with them and enjoyed feeling repeatedly repulsed.

The stockboy liked to talk, but not many people apart from Tracy were willing to listen to him. He sat on her desk spinning a blue plastic lighter and described a scene from *The Bride of Frankenstein* in which tiny creatures—a king, a queen, a ballerina, and others—were created and kept in bell jars. Some of the things they sell here, he said to Tracy, aren't far from little live freaks in glass jars. The stockboy had been in the museum upstairs only once, so his idea of what was exhibited there was based on the contents of crates and invoices fanning out from clipboards. The museum he constructed from this evidence was a sort of circus with a Gothic cast. Tracy went back to her reading. She felt sorry for him, but he was beginning to get on her nerves.

> Margaret of Valois was married to Henry, the Protestant king of Navarre. The wedding had been symbolic. It was arranged as a gesture of peace between Protestants and Catholics. Her infidelities began only as rumors, but her correspondence confirmed her affairs, and she would not stop writing. She made copies of the letters she sent and kept the ones she received. When various halves of her correspondence fell into the wrong hands, her promiscuity became public and she was sent into exile. Estranged from her court, she organized resistance against her husband and brother, but they captured the queen and locked her up. She was jealous of her husband's mistress and would not grant him an annulment even after she was released from prison.

A secretary shared her office. She had pictures of her wedding on a Rolodex. She could spin it so fast the ceremony appeared like a movie in which the secretary had been director, star, and scriptwriter. For one day she had been all of these. Bridesmaids in blue hats, the best man, the ring bearer and flower girl all spun by as Tracy twirled the secretary's nameless Rolodex.

To Tracy's annoyance the secretary had also gotten into the habit of staying in for lunch as well. Perhaps because of the record cold temperatures no one wanted to go out, but Tracy missed her privacy. The stockboy looked in and asked them if they wanted anything from the cafeteria. The secretary asked for cigarettes. She had saved a tiny dough-nut from a tray the museum put out every morning as a Christmas gesture. They were free, but by noon even the chocolate-covered ones were hard and dried up. She found this habit irritating as well.

Every time she lifted the receiver, the secretary stopped typing. Tracy suspected she was listening to her telephone calls. She became self-conscious and told the stockboy she was being watched. He didn't believe her.

"Why would anyone be interested in you?"

"Think of speech as a form of letter writing," she said to the stockboy in exasperation, "and the secretary has been asked to open outgoing mail."

She made up a conversation about her wallet being stolen at the movies, but this time the secretary typed through her anxiety about money that hadn't really been lost at all.

She invented conspiracy theories as if she were trying to overthrow her brother, still a prince in an unnamed Never-Never Land, when in fact he now worked as an orderly in a hospital where he feared there was a bed somewhere with his name on it. Or, she was Tracy of Valois who had married the wrong man. In one conversation, she would deny all liaisons, in another she would describe each meeting, each narrow escape. The only result of Tracy's fictions was that the secretary, in her effort to disguise her eavesdropping, thought she was carrying on with the stockboy and started to give her advice. Tracy gave up the simulated conversations and began to describe her actual circumstances just as she would have done if she weren't being listened to. Her job in the basement of the museum was temporary and when it ended, she anticipated lying in bed each morning and wait-ing for the employment agency to call. If the telephone hadn't rung by nine o'clock, she'd try to fall back to sleep and pick up on dreams that ended abruptly, but they never repeated themselves. She was never in the same hotel or with the same people, and she rarely recognized anyone. The characters in her dreams were all vague composites. Over the telephone, at work, she complained to a friend that the Christmas rush was ending, and those mornings would begin soon. The secretary resumed typing.

Rats and mice started to get into the basement, eating the books and reproductions. Their droppings fell out of gold jewelry wrapped in tissue and bright silk scarves, printed reproductions. The stockboy was assigned the job of plugging up the holes. In the evening Tracy could hear rats scratching behind the wall. She had read about scratching heard in Rome after the Germans evacuated. A few Nazis had remained behind, hiding in crypts under the city. British and American GIs found what appeared to be simple plans of the crypts and went to look for the lost Germans. Priests who had been collaborationists tried to stop them but the Allies removed the priests and went in anyway. They discovered that the crypts were not simple. They were full of alleys and abysses dating back to the ninth century. The map was useless, and they finally gave up the search.

"They really want to get in here, whoever's clawing so frantically," she said.

"This is New York. It's just rats," said the stockboy, and he complained that management kept telling him to plug up more holes, a hopeless task in the vast basement.

When she worked evenings, Tracy thought of the lost soldiers sending signals. No one has told them they've made it to New York and that particular war is over.

THE SECRETARY began to suspect Tracy was taking books home. She didn't want to rat but became very icy toward her. The secretary no longer liked working in the basement and wanted a promotion upstairs where people were better dressed, although she knew they weren't the kind of people who put their wedding pictures on Rolodexes. As a permanent employee, she thought she deserved to get out of the basement and would do what she could to improve her chances. Tracy was not like the secretary. She had brought no photographs with her to work. When she left for the day her desk was relatively empty except for the blue bear the stockboy had given her. When the toy fell apart, which it did promptly, she glued its arms and legs onto her telephone with a hot glue gun. It wasn't a very messy operation and even gave the thing an anthropomorphic cast. The stockboy laughed at the bear/phone but her superiors were neither pleased nor offered to give it to her when she was asked to leave. The basement and sub-basement were full of relics and reproductions, and she liked to think that the telephone, too, would be wrapped up and found by someone else next year. A clerk rearranging the out-of-print books would discover the adulterous and unhappy Margarets were missing and what had been put in their place were pieces of newspaper whose stories ran straight across the page.

Incunabula #3

PEOPLE USED TO read everything as if it were a story. Readers looked for moral tales. They wanted to be taught a lesson and then to move on to the next potential mistake. They matched accidents and natural disasters to hearsay, fables, and myths. It was a way of imposing logic on mishaps. It initiated a system of cross-referential meaning where none would seem to have existed previously. It was a way to avoid appearing like a city of helpless victims hit by random catastrophe. Here was authority. Here was a motive for revenge. People used to read for pleasure. People wanted to recognize the end of a story in its beginning. People wanted to be surprised at its end, anyway.

SHE GREW increasingly afraid to leave her apartment and gave others complicated grocery lists. When they were uncooperative, she would live on coffee with powdered milk and spaghetti sauce eaten directly from the jar with a spoon. Her personal geography grew truncated in proportion to potential fatalities that she associated with runaway subway cars and the crimes she linked to the density of foreigners in the streets. She defined a foreigner as anyone she failed to recognize. The hazards crept toward the door. She would listen to the radio for hours as a substitute for actually doing anything. She approached the act of listening the way another person might consider driving a car or writing a letter. Radio time began to replace clock time. The news came on five minutes before twelve. That divided the morning into equal parts but added five minutes to the first hour of the afternoon. Friends hoped she might have some reconciliation with at least the front steps of her building before the end of the summer.

I SEE THEM working in subways. Blue, green, gold, orange tiles: the front of a locomotive, little houses unlike any seen in metropolitan New York, beavers and squirrels in profile. Each piece has been previously cut to the right shape. There is a signal and they jump onto the platform. They mainly work at night. In the morning a gold stripe, a red bracket, sort of baroque, or a tree has been added. Everything is finally covered by something, there is no space left undecorated. When their work is completed, the tilers move on to another station. The irregularity of their presence during daylight and the danger of their work make them seem like peripatetic tap dancers who put together a different act each night. Even after the signal they behave as if they have all the time in the world. One of them noticed I was missing trains in order to watch them so I got on the next one. Later in the night, after they've gone home, painters come and cover parts of the tiles with tags and pictures. There are ghost stations, entirely painted over, which the train passes between working stops. Sometimes the cars halt in front of one; dimly lit and long out of service. It might move slowly past a series of stations full of pictures: an early form of cinema. In the future all stations will be painted over and all the trains will be slow express trains: the history of cinema advances. A movie with images of trailing comets, rockets, larger-than-life silver letters takes shape. Historically earlier parts will feature words made of bubble letters, in later ones the letters turn angular. This has been called Gothic Futurism. In the depths of each station colored names will give way to jungle landscapes, images of mechanized monsters, caricatures of comic figures. Sequences mimic existing perspectives to such an extent that people will be sure they must have missed a corner as the train passes. They will want to repeat the trip, in effect, see the movie again. Even though there is so much to see, tiers of scenery, the train must keep up a certain speed or the effect of animation will be lost.

IT HAD ONCE been exciting to be identified, named, and photographed. This happened to her mother in 1939 when she was eleven and the family was broke. Her mother got a job as Mrs. Modern at the World's Fair in Queens. She worked opposite Mrs. Drudge in the Westinghouse Pavilion. Every morning she put on her costume and went to work. Her picture was in papers and newsreels whenever the Westinghouse Pavilion was discussed. Sometimes she was by herself, sometimes she was photographed with Mrs. Drudge who had no machines and did everything by hand. The whirligig of sensationalism occasionally included the actual sons and daughters of Mrs. Modern and Mrs. Drudge as they went through their daily lives as real children. A *Life* photographer appeared at her school looking for her. She ducked into the bathroom, spent a few hours there, then ran away. She didn't want to be recognized as a child of Mrs. Modern.

BECAUSE SHE had so little information, written language was all she would trust. Words spread out like puddles of inference, thin at the edges, creeping toward misuse, misspelling, mispronunciation. The boundaries of words grew vague. One impersonated the next. She set up a schemata based on analogous relationships.

All hotels have a few rules in common.
Everyone needs the right clothes.
You must have money in order to live.
Repulsive behavior can take many forms.

She read newspaper lines straight across: "the women wear full length mink major source of permanent housing for the homeless can't ski anywhere in the world without a gold Rolex. Official said the city hoped would not set foot without major gemstones, $49 a day for a family of four"

"It ruined a three-week trip. forced to leave buildings that have been abandoned.
Still other had to leave overcrowded apartments of"

" 'comes a guy with the latest Italian skiwear. I was proud. I told him,
ments more quickly. Homeless families are now housed in hotels"

"You don't stay in a hotel, you stay in a
what-do-you-call-it? A house."

Iterative clauses hinted at branches of connotation and so she made diagrams. Antiphrasis struck deaf ears. She had no sense of irony. She read literally and lines of print gave her a hard time. She became easily distracted, turned to another page, confronted a similar set of lines, felt hungry, struck a match, lit a burner and boiled water. It was all as discontinuous as the definition of hotel.

YOU HAD TO know someone or be with someone who knew someone in order to get in. A narrow storefront, almost not that, almost a corridor connecting other corridors that you really couldn't get into. Sometimes there were a couple of tables and chairs inside. Sometimes a man (it was not always a man) or two would be sitting in one of them. If you just walked in off the street the fat guy behind the counter would tell you in Spanish that they weren't open for business.

A man I knew was like Mr. Memory in *The Thirty-nine Steps*. He would take risks if you could manage to convince him no one would guess what he was really doing. No one would believe his intentions were anything but benign, his interests anything but self-interests. He didn't appear the sort of person easily waylaid by aimless curiosity. I persuaded him to go in with me because I couldn't go in by myself. I would be nervous, my teeth would chatter, I would look at the floor. Like Mr. Memory, he would know the answers to their questions and if they, like the German spies in the movie, asked for the formula for a particular airplane engine, he would have recited arbitrary numbers and I'm sure they would have been the correct ones. Neither one of us did get in. I never found out what went on in there.

Like Madeleine Carroll, I didn't want to be attached to the stranger who kissed her/me on the train. As danger became more apparent, she became more cooperative, but in my case, the danger was of my own invention. If we were Madeleine Carroll and Robert Donat handcuffed together, rolling down an embankment, playing elopers at a hotel, then he couldn't be Mr. Memory at the same time. Hero and traitor mixed in the same actor. Possibly the story was skewed. I felt stuck into the wrong character.

HE DIDN'T recognize her. He was sitting at a table with other people, looked up at her and then spoke to his friends as if she were no one in particular. She walked close to the group as if she were going to the telephone booth to their right. He didn't look up. She pretended to make a call, put a quarter in the slot and dialed her own number, left a message for herself on the machine. The message made little sense and continued long past the beep. The cord was very long for a phone booth. She turned, winding it around herself so she was facing him, but he still didn't recognize her or even notice her. He was wearing a tie with silver horseshoes and horses' heads painted on it. From where she stood the horse heads looked like shiny flies. An unknown woman wrapped in a telephone cord, like Jane Avril wrapped in a snake. She thought she should have made up a conversation instead of leaving a long message on what was actually her own machine but it was too late to change her story. As if anyone who might hear her would stop their own conversation and ask her just what kind of a nut she thought she was. He tapped the table to make a point, then looked out the window as if disgusted or defeated. She couldn't go on just standing there.

THE PERSONAL things put on each desk grew to monstrous representations of buffoonery. The ashtray with *My Favorite Martian*'s picture embedded in it says goofiness is the large category under which you operate. Even actions committed for sincere reasons, under serious pretense, will prove just as embarrassing. The ashtray denies all of this. Your motives can never rise any higher. Other employees have feminized objects on their desks: artificial flowers, birthday cards, picture frames, souvenir lighters. You can't say if these objects are feminized or emasculated because, conceptually, they are relatively neuter. They could have gone either way. A lighter or the idea of a lighter wasn't originally burdened by connotations of gender, at least not in English. A man in the office suggests these objects are emasculated by virtue of combination. He has a paperweight of the Empire State Building embedded in plastic on his desk. When you shake the thing, of course, it snows. The paperweight might be a cliché but he insists it's not femmey. No one suggests to him that the World Trade Center is bigger. I go to another floor to get a cup of coffee out of a fairly neutral-looking machine. I find myself being drawn to the image of cuteness in inert things, but if you relinquish everything to cuteness, you might become happy enough at your job so that you would think twice before leaving it.

She wrote *rue*. No further description was needed. *Rue* was not the same as *rua, via,* or street. She wrote Eldridge in front of street, *rue* needed no modifier. It already spoke of balconies, thin curtains, a set of shutters which opened out and a pair of windows which opened in.

Eventually only printed language which had been reproduced had any credibility. She felt like a caretaker of inauthentic documents and she was in search of a nucleus of the original sentence. They were fly-by-night resurrections, none of them to be entirely trusted. Tokens: the resurrections were only traces of some past myth of precision. She had no faith in pictures or photographs. All evidence had to be verbal. She kept stacks of newspapers in mostly chronological order. It was a slow system. She couldn't always find what she was looking for. Her hands and cuffs were often dirty, her forehead smeared with inky tracks.

One subject that never, to her knowledge, appeared in print was her own life. Even its most mundane aspects were never verified by reproduction in newspapers. The stacks under tables and chairs, under her bed, suggested an important simulation and one that excluded her.

He told me a story about finding a human hand in a garbage can. I didn't believe him. I know people who find decent furniture and remarkable clothing on the street, but a human hand, never. He was putting off going back to his apartment and would just say anything. He did this every night after work. I asked him what kind of hand it was, what did it look like? Black or white, big or little? Was it holding anything? Was it wearing jewelry? I didn't exactly make a study of it, he said. How do you know if it was real at all? Maybe it was rubber. No, it was real, this was no rubber hand, he was certain. Did you go to the police? No, there was no point, it was just a hand, not a body. Could it have been a prop? You said it wasn't rubber but it might have been something else, some special kind of plastic, for example. Were you walking near a theater or a prop shop? He was getting annoyed but he didn't want to go home. There are cities where things like this happen and it is considered normal. You don't have to live in Santiago or Buenos Aires to find body parts on the street. But this, I reminded him, is not one of those cities.

Had the hand taken over his life? Had its appearance ruined for him further use? Well, yes, for a few days he had been upset and thought of little else. He couldn't put a plastic bag full of coffee grounds and balled-up pieces of paper—a bag which said "Have a Nice Day!"—on top of a human hand.

He didn't want to go inside his building yet. It was warm and after we separated I knew he'd walk around for hours. If we hadn't worked together that night he would have attached himself to someone else or roamed the street talking to himself.

PEOPLE HAVE always found before-and-after stories very compelling. The lives of formerly bald, now hairy, or formerly fat, now thin people are automatically read as stories because they prove that anyone can start a new life, regardless of the past. People used to read as a substitute for religion. People used to read if they were patricians. People used to read everything as if it were a metaphor, or if not that, as if all the lines contained nothing but tropes. People used to put off the end of the story for as long as possible, putting obstacles between it and the moment at hand, even if they knew how the story would end, and had known its end since they could remember.

Scissors and Rocks

"Scissors and Rocks" was written for the "Rhetorical Image" show presented at the New Museum of Contemporary Art, New York (December 1991), and was published in the exhibition catalogue.

Sentences and phrases set in the same sans serif typeface as this headnote are Bertolt Brecht's or Walter Benjamin's own words, as quoted in "Walter Benjamin: Conversations with Brecht," in *Aesthetics and Politics,* edited by Fredric Jameson (Verso, 1980). The illustration on page 167, *The Battle of the Strong Boxes and the Money Bags* by Ione Galle, after Brueghel the Elder, is reproduced courtesy Baker Library, Harvard Business School.

WATER COURSED DOWN grooves defining the muscles of his useless bronze horse and dripped from his curly, verdigris-coated wig. The statue of Eugene, Duke of Savoy, looked blue and green in the rain. A few windows had been shattered in the night, and fragments of glass lay scattered on the pavement. Indifferent to the weather, Benjamin kicked the shards ahead of him. He looked in at a newsstand which sold foreign newspapers, and it occurred to him as he turned away that that small square contained all of Europe in a badly lit box. From the darkened stairwell of a narrow building, he heard German, Russian, and Czech coming from the closed doors above. He listened closely, but heard no metaphors, no rhymes, no onomatopoeic jokes. The words were not used expressively; they were meant to represent exactly the objects or actions they referred to. Eugene had freed the Turkish women of the Sultan's harem, taken them to Vienna and, given their liberty in the city, they were imprisoned by linguistic isolation. They slept beside his bronze horse and laughed at his frozen waves of Bernini-ish hair. They scratched their names in the bronze turf under the horse's hooves, only to have the Arabic polished away when they moved on to another piece of public sculpture or statuary in the morning.

Benjamin remembered Brecht saying something—an argument for or against censorship, or possibly a certain person's speech or manner—was like the re-blocking of an old felt hat for the two-thousandth time, and he could imagine a soft gray hat vainly pressed over a steamy mold, but what it was analogous to, he had forgotten. He wandered toward the Orient Cinémathèque. Three cheers for darkened rooms, André Breton had said, and late though it was, Benjamin paid for a ticket and went inside. As he entered the theater, John Barrymore was arranging to have Carole Lombard followed by a detective. The *Twentieth Century* half over, Benjamin thought, "This is where I come in." Loudly and irritably, the actor sneered, "When Ira Jaffe says the Iron Door closes, the Iron Door closes," and with his hand, he slammed a great, imaginary door shut. The audience laughed. The movie ended, and the theater closed. Ushers didn't see Benjamin as they locked the door. He put his feet up on the empty seat in front of him and tried to reconstruct Paper, Scissors, and Rocks.

July 6, 1934

Brecht, in the course of yesterday's conversations: "I often imagine being interrogated by a tribunal. 'Now tell us, Mr. Brecht, are you really in earnest?' I would have to admit that no, I'm not really in earnest. I think too much about artistic problems."

He wrote leaning against the seatback in front of him. In the darkened Orient, it was difficult to remember the details of Brecht's sickroom. He could picture Brecht sitting up in bed parroting his accuser, Now tell us. . . . Red-eyed and coughing, he had looked minatory. Brecht's mimicry of the imaginary future tribunal had occurred in the middle of their conversation and, although Brecht had said that he thought his position and his defense permissible, he had conceded neither were really very effective. In Brecht's pallor, Benjamin had seen himself on some future witness stand, unable to say anything. Uncomfortable, he had looked up. The words *Truth is concrete* decorated the ceiling. He wondered how Brecht, ill and complaining of dizziness, had managed to paint them so neatly. Other words, runelike, were difficult to make out. Benjamin had squinted. Diacritic marks covered the ceiling like a kind of linguistic constellation. Settling all four chair legs on the floor, he returned his gaze to Brecht, who was drinking a glass of water. Waiting, Benjamin studied a small wooden donkey with a jointed, nodding head sitting on the windowsill beside him. A sign hung round its neck read, "Even I must understand." The writing again was Brecht's. He picked up the donkey to see how the head was attached. The painted sign was suspended from a small hook screwed into its neck.

"Lenin wouldn't write a novel," Brecht said, as he took another drink of water. "People would laugh. Suppose you read a very good historical novel and later you discover that it is by Lenin. You would change your opinion of both, to the detriment of both."

The world, Brecht felt, was divided into two kinds of cultural producers, just two: "the visionary artist" and "the cool-headed, thinking man who is not completely in earnest." He claimed to have a foot in both camps. He had said, after all, that he was not completely in earnest, but Benjamin decided to ignore the contradiction. If he liked to think of himself as a con artist, Benjamin was willing to humor him. The two categories seemed to form a pair, a social dyad, inseparable. Two things that went hand in glove, Brecht might have said to defend himself.

Benjamin, giving the donkey head another knock, asked, "And Kafka? Which one is he?"

"Kafka had only one problem: he was terrified of the empire of

ants. He never found a solution. He never woke from his nightmare."

A foot jerked from under the sheets. He seemed agitated.
Perhaps he was not as confident as he appeared. With its
hidden labyrinths and unspeakable, stinging authorities, the
city built of mud crumbs was one of his nightmares as well.

"Look at it this way," Benjamin said. "I'll invent a conversation between myself and Kafka, the sort of conversation we might have if he were here now. And so, while you
were busy formulating dyads or putting drops in your eyes, I
might start by asking Kafka if he has a horror of organizations,
property relations, and the language of economics. I don't
think we should ask him about insects."

"You don't have to tell me," Brecht said. "When asked if
reference to anything financial induces apprehension, anxiety, or the shakes, K. would, of course, nod in agreement."

"A share certificate fills you with dread?"

"K. would certainly agree with that, too. The problem
is that K. is looking for an arthropode leader, a Queen Bee,
an Ant Chair, and they're all bad news. Pooh-bahs, essentially."

"Kafka is certain of the frailty of all safeguards?" Benjamin asked.

"There is that frailty, the stigmata of paranoia, and he
cowers behind an assertion of precariousness, that's all."

"He keeps tunneling anyway?"

"Tunneling in place."

HIS FOOT disappeared under the sheet again, and he offered
to explain the dyad in the form of an allegory.

"Imagine two writers who go about their business in different and often antagonistic ways." The construction was
more of a tetrad, he said, because he was going to include
himself as overseer and Benjamin as a spectator. He got up,
walked to his desk, and moved glasses, medicine, and books

to one side as if he were clearing a stage. A nonsense tetrad, the spectator thought.

"We'll call one of these invented writers Scissors and the other one Rocks." He paused. "I'll be Paper. Surely Paper will come out of this on top."

"Are they men or women?" Benjamin asked.

"Men, of course."

"Are they German?"

"Yes, I think they'd have to be."

Scissors is composing a satirical novel, *Herr Julius Caesar, Himself.* Afraid that if he writes the word *lassitude,* he will become what an American detective story writer once called a two-fisted loafer, he is very careful about his fiction. He so identifies with his characters that the fear of actually becoming one of them never leaves him. Julius Caesar, *c'est moi,* he explains.

"As you might imagine, Rocks groans," Brecht said, "at the pretension. Still, his suspicions are aroused. If Scissors writes words like *cannibal, plagiarist, namedropper, social climber,* or even simple *envy,* will he take on these personas, attributes, and neuroses?"

Rocks is writing a play, The Business Affairs of Herr Julius Caesar, a cycle of scenes which deals with life under fascism. It is very realistic, following what Brecht called Pattern X: coffee cups are coffee cups, meat and potatoes meat and potatoes; objects are literally what they are. Symbolism is not their province. The situation is resolved by whatever elements are on the stage during the first scene; nothing new is introduced. Rocks, a practitioner of Pattern X, looks at Brueghel for lessons on realism. He points to *The Battle of the Strong Boxes and the Money Bags* as a critical lesson on the spiraling obsession of avarice. Heads, nearly smothered in coins, poke out of the tops of bags and those in the background look as if they have been transmogrified into clumps of change. Rocks speaks of aggression looked at through the lens of metaphor, as a critique of the distribution of capital. Scissors says he can't work this way. Transmogrification, he leers, still smarting at the contempt elicited by his *c'est moi,* means humor, grotesquerie, and he doesn't see it. The picture is chaotic, a chess game turned upside down in the middle of a tornado. The money bags have arms and legs. They don't really look like money bags, and a picture of bags and boxes is no attack on capital as far as he can tell.

When Scissors looks at Brueghel, he feels bombarded; the joke eludes him. When he sees the skinny *magerman* in the Fat Kitchen, the allegorical interloper who presents a moral test to the spectator, he wants to shout, All right, already! Just eat the pie. "After all, the moral test isn't my problem; it's a test for those two-dimensional flatties stuffing chickens and roasting lambs. I'm not in the picture, don't forget."

Pictures that socially anthologize, showing every manner of virtue, reward, crime, and punishment, those images, moldy and antique, give him a headache. Scissors wants a collection of small, private moments, no indiscriminate global topography, no panopticon from prime ministers to sweeps.

Scissors combs his hair in a small mirror he carries. He watches his reflection, faceted, multiplied, or distorted, as he passes cafés. He studies himself in shop windows, imagining his head hovering over the collars of sharp suits displayed on decapitated dummies. His clothes are shabby. It's not his life, but he wedges his head between each hatstand and its fedora, each homburg crowns his imaginary aspirations. Where there was only a shadow and dust motes before, the space is now occupied by the head of Scissors. He writes down the conversations he struggles so hard to overhear, straining and trying, at the same time, to look busy elsewhere. He doesn't want to appear to be eavesdropping. He looks in ground-floor apartment windows when the light blots his reflections out and records what he sees: meals, gestures of impatience, undone clothes, dishes left in the sink. He tries not to be malicious in his transcription of what he calls small lives. His notebook voices seem very accurate, their characters able to enter a room and conduct themselves in a lifelike manner. He moves them around with ease, engineering their meetings. They might enjoy each other or argue, sometimes refuse to speak, and sometimes he sends them into the bedroom, where he looks through the keyhole, taking notes again.

Rocks is short of time. He races around the city, photographing and taping every possible moment. He discards his police radio with its broadcasts of on-the-spot explosions; these are not his kinds of crimes, although they have their flashy side. He finds felony and social transgression everywhere, in big arenas and small, and he is usually on target. Rocks's files are overflowing with information which will find its way into his play. He catalogues evidence of stalking-horses he feels he has tracked in his observations of presidential and mayoral radio speeches, double features, newsreels, and a man who beats his girlfriend under Rocks's window late one night. A vacuum cleaner with a bent for agit-prop, he sucks up all kinds of content, eventually plugging most of the pieces into his constructions. When he occasionally sees some of Scissors's shadow people, he manipulates them to his purposes. Someday, Scissors tells him, he may learn the difference between moral and moralistic, and goes back to his keyhole. When he photographs only women, Scissors accuses him of believing in parthenogenetic humans. "The photographed universe you've created is a lopsided copy of all of this!" Scissors waves his hands and pounds the table in front of him, causing glasses to jump. When he photographs only men, Scissors slaps him on the back, but is quickly disillusioned with what Rocks has done. The pictures are in fragments and some are written over. In spite of the bits and pieces, Scissors knows that these are the kind of men who say, "In reference to certain moneys," plural, rather than, "Do you have any?" Kafka, had he been in the audience, would smell a rat. These men, caught in the act, didn't look so good, but Scissors reasons that it might not make any difference. Rocks's pictures won't change a thing, he says to his reflection.

Paper crosses his arms and looks at both of them like a caretaker who has just bopped a pair of moles on the head. Pictures are scattered across the floor. Leaning over to get a closer look, he pokes Rocks's photographs, specimens of lost possibilities, with the end of a pen. He must bend very far, which he does with difficulty.

"Both of you have only produced a kind of meta-existence with all these representations," Paper says, as if reading Benjamin's mind. "This spectacle, or these spectacles," he looks in the direction of Rocks and Scissors, "isn't an ordered collection of images, but a whirligig for mediating social relations between various parties who, under ordinary circumstances, wouldn't know a thing about one another's flight patterns. The psychological effect of the experience of all these accumulated representations has conditioned some to prefer the sensational desire stimulated by the representations over the actual experience or thing itself." Rocks feels as if he has been wrapped up and undone.

Thumbing through Scissors's notebook, Paper shrugs, then lets it fall to the floor in a gesture of hammered boredom. Little lives, small domestic moments, claustrophobic and turned in on themselves, Who cares? He accents the last syllable with particular ennui and stuffs chewing gum into the keyhole. Deeply affronted, Scissors howls that he has been blinded, then, aping blurred vision, extends his arms before him like a sleepwalker. Suddenly he stops and, as if someone has pushed a button somewhere, his eyelids, like shades, snap up. If this is his way of protesting the blockage, the Spectator is sure something is afoot. Perhaps it is that Scissors is not afraid of Paper. Scissors can cut. He drops to his stomach, pushes his glasses up the bridge of his nose, and writes furiously in his fallen notebook. Paper, however, ignores him. He is, after all, thick.

"I'm not against the asocial, you know; I'm against the non-social," Rocks pipes up from the corner into which he has rolled. Paper and Scissors show no interest. Though all his attempts at sincerity have turned into pratfalls, he musters a last shred of dignity. His tone turns formal. "Someday," he announces, "I'm going to write an encyclopedic survey of the follies of the Tellectual-Ins, called Tui. It will have an enormous number of entries, arranged chronologically rather than alphabetically, and will read as a work of fiction, although every word should be true." On hearing this, the Spectator had not been certain to what extent he ought to play an absorbed audience and to what extent he should heckle or note

Brecht's duplicity. During a conversation they had had on Baudelaire the night before, Brecht had made exactly the same statement and described an identical encyclopedia. It was an obvious ruse, making Rocks his mouthpiece instead of taking responsibility for some of his own ideas. Benjamin decided he wouldn't let him get away with it. These words, he had whispered hoarsely, should not be attributed to Rocks because they were Brecht's own.

"I'm Spectator," he recorded himself saying. "And I do remember."

Scissors, in the meantime, was glowering as if great offense were being taken. Whatever Rocks and Paper had to say was nothing he cared to record, and the contorted expression on his face caused Rocks to wonder what plots for revenge were percolating inside him. While Scissors seemed to listen silently, Rocks didn't trust appearances. Clamping his limbs together so that he stood up very straight, Scissors snapped that he considered namedropping a form of shoplifting authority. Rocks glared back and reminded him that even under wraps, he, Rocks, was capable of bone-splitting damage if pushed too far.

Sidling up to Paper menacingly, Scissors said, "I'm suspicious of the words *utility, sovereignty, sanctity;* and we know that the concept of nationality has a quite particular, sacramental, pompous and suspicious connotation." Paper fired back that those were the exact words of the Spectator and not very original.

Turning to Benjamin, Paper said, "Talking to them is like shooting ducks in a barrel. Let's leave them." He was clearly feeling that his dyad was getting out of hand. "I have another story that might interest you." But the Spectator enjoyed listening to Brecht's mimicry and was loath to abandon this reconstruction of it.

Brecht took on another role. He stood in front of Benjamin's chair and claimed to be "the State." Noting later that he looked sly, cunning, furtive, and gave sidelong glances to an imaginary interlocutor, Benjamin saw that this impersonation was the most abstract and terrifying yet. The State seemed to fill the room like a Disney-inspired shadow and, alone in the theater, Benjamin again remembered how uneasy Brecht had made him feel. To change the subject, he had said that he was no longer interested in being Spectator, but didn't feel up to the task of spectacle either; that was Brecht's skill. He couldn't pretend to speak in the voice of the State, Scissors, or Paper. Brecht, looking pleased, sat down on his bed and dropped his last role of the evening.

"Are these the elements of Pattern X?" Benjamin asked. "A wooden animal, a bottle of pills, Scissors looking through the window, and Rocks not far behind? If so, there's no place in your system for an imaginary state."

"Sometimes Pattern X isn't the answer. The prevailing aesthetic, the price of books, and the police have always ensured that there is a considerable distance between writer and people."

But who are the *police* in that sentence? Benjamin shifted in his seat. The guises and long arm of the pooh-bahs can take fantastic, as well as predictable, forms.

ONE OF THE ushers had accidentally left a light on near the far outer aisle. Originally a baroque theater, the Orient seemed in competition with the American movies shown on its screen. During the screening, Benjamin had enjoyed letting his eyes wander from the figures of Thalia, Artemis, Pan, and Mercury to the flat image of a man sending a telegram or a train hurtling through a tunnel. Even if he wanted to, he couldn't sleep. The armrests were worn and a dim light bounced off the gilt balconies. He found the projection booth, its door open, and flipped a switch. Light filled the small room, some spilling into the theater. Peering through the window between booth and audience, he saw several figures slumped in chairs, writing in notebooks or talking to themselves. One turned round to look in the direction of the light, as if to determine the source of the disturbance. He stared through Benjamin's face in the window and then went back to his writing.

X ≠ Y

Your passport was something you needed to get on the airplane in the first place. It was blue, it meant a statistical affiliation, not something you gave a lot of thought to. The picture of George Washington, like a crucifix, or a crèche in the neighbors' houses, signs you easily identified, knew all about, completely understood; but these things weren't in the house you remember. They were foreign, exiled objects. As a daughter of bearers of different passports you didn't share the neighbors' matter-of-fact, wake-up-you're-it heritage. *Heritage* is a word which, like the word *leadership*, makes you uneasy. The only time you tasted Bosco or Reddi-Whip was somewhere else. The idea of nationality may be a received one, but with so many generations born in exactly the same place, it's taken for granted. Your passport says you have a connection to all these things (a garage with a basketball hoop over a barn red door, a jockey on someone's lawn) that you walked past without noticing.

History class, 1966, open *Eurasia*. All year you memorized products, imports, exports, natural resources from Ireland to Korea. You were eleven. It was called history, but this is what you commit to memory, a different country each week. What were the products of Iraq? Petroleum, raw wool, and dates. These are exports. Of Ireland? Live animals, imports are machinery, petroleum. The map in your textbook stopped dead in the middle of Europe and picked up again with Greece. It was a book of very few dates; history was not considered to have a temporal dimension.

The men in black masks who have appeared at the front of the plane aren't interested in how you saw through your history teachers or that there is a copy of *The Eighteenth Brumaire of Louis Bonaparte* in your suitcase. Everything you think of sounds ridiculous and naive. The man next to you says he thinks you will be exchanged for prisoners held in another country but he's only guessing.

They find a place to land, and although you are sitting near a window, you can't identify the city. None of the passengers are allowed to speak.

A spokesman for the Italian Ministry, Tanino Scelba, said Wednesday that a "terrorist multinational" exists and argued that you cannot speak of isolated groups, like the Brigata Rosa or the Red Army faction. They are linked, he said.

The terrorist multinational does not have links to the Trilateral Commission. The syllogism falls on its face.

AIRPLANE DETRITUS, trays of melted ice, tiny whiskey and gin bottles roll on the floor, there will be no seconds, silent headphones dangle around people's necks. The movie, *Greystoke,* was an old one, but you didn't rent sound. Ape-man swings through the jungle in utter quiet. The flight attendants are asked to push the screens back up, but for some reason the movie continues and images of lianas, Tarzan's long hair and legs flash across the women's faces as they make a last trip down the aisles. You and the stranger sitting by the aisle can only look at each other. Perhaps it's just as well you aren't allowed to speak. You look for the signs which will tell you what speech, in this situation, can't. Is he reading *Der Spiegel* or *People* magazine in Dutch? A newspaper whose Cyrillic figures you're unable to understand? When called to the front and faced with the interpreter, what story will he give? He owns things, cuff links, briefcase, tie pin, with his initials on them. You look for a Rolex, but even if he's wearing one it could be a fake bought on the street. You aren't in a Hitchcock movie scattered with these kinds of clues. You don't fall in love.

Hands are supposed to be raised when you want to use the bathroom. Will one of them go in with you or will you be searched before? Will speech on a limited basis creep back because, after a certain number of hours, if people aren't really terrorized, attempts to communicate with one another may be undertaken surreptitiously until the rhythms of talking slowly gain momentum, and you are threatened into silence once more? You remember what it's like to be afraid to open your mouth. You think two of them are women.

There are passengers you saw as you boarded the plane who looked like the kind of people who would say anything to save themselves, not knowing their inventions would fail. What are the signs of this kind of resourcefulness? You remember a lot of gold jewelry and some fuss about seats. These people might grow confused and babble under interrogation, but it isn't clear what anyone might say in order to get off the plane anyway. After passports have been collected, some passengers are asked what they do for a living. The interpreter is a passenger who seemed to have volunteered out of the blue, although you can see from the expressions of the people around you he is viewed with suspicion. He might not know the languages in question very well and might make up answers for you. He acts a little nervous, but it's a histrionic kind of nervousness as if he's sure he has a job to do and feels himself to be on neutral ground, at least for the time being. You can see categories being assessed. You wonder who's worth what to them. You stretch your neck looking for diplomats, movie stars, CIA operatives.

"Don't take me, take her."

IN SCHOOL you read about the *Bristol Constant,* a boat of little interest, without treasure or intrigue at first. It was on its way to the Massachusetts Bay Colony when the crew mutinied off the coast of Newfoundland. Bullets weren't wasted. Men and women were thrown overboard into the icy water. The mutinous crew was forbidden landing in any English port and was forced to resort to piracy. One woman was kept, although she pleaded to be sent back to England on the next east-sailing ship they attacked. She talked of Brighton day and night. The mutineers thought she was mad and left her on the barren, unpopulated shore of an island in the West Indies.

IT HAS BEEN two days or a day and a half. You can't really tell. You realize that even before you boarded this plane you spent a lot of time waiting. Watch time is a form of nonsense, a form of abstract speculation, because the time where you came from no longer has any meaning. You try to remember newspaper stories of amnesty and happy endings but can recall no complete stories, only what the front pages of various newspapers look like. You hear someone having a hysterical conversation with themselves several rows behind you. The person, who is left alone and allowed his or her monologues, is playing all the roles in the conversation, and you find it disturbing that you can't stand up in order to identify the speaker. You don't even know if it's a man or a woman. Everyone is awake. If rumors could circulate in a silence you're not sure you would really know anything more.

THEY WANT four Polisarios freed from a Moroccan jail.

They want Italian prisoners held in "preventive detention" returned to ordinary life.

They want enough fuel to fly to East Berlin.

They want half the Vatican's treasure.

They want the men to sit on one side of the plane, the women on the other.

No one will get their passport back.

AIRPLANE FOOD runs out. Trays are wheeled across the tarmac. When it is distributed, the food gives no clues as to the country you've landed in. Long thawed peas and carrots, microwaved french fries, Swiss steak, a cupcake for dessert.

There is agitation among those watching the passengers. One of the others who has been behind the curtain comes forward, and they speak in a language you can't identify. Tremendous amounts of film, video tape, and print might be generated outside the perimeters of your captivity. Mountains of lights, cameras, and extension cords approach the control tower, shredded newspapers eddy near the wheels of the plane.

In your boredom, it's easy to panic, but have no way to demonstrate your alarm except to raise your hand to go to the bathroom. You are ignored and in your desperation turn to the stranger with monograms who has fallen asleep. Unless he secretly took some drug in the bathroom, you don't understand how he can sleep, awkwardly falling into the empty seat between you. In sleep he looks like he might be watching a movie, listening to a concert, or dreaming in an undisturbed manner, and you're envious of his oblivion. He has very white teeth.

They are looking at passports again, dividing them into stacks according to color. You can't see if they're looking at yours, if they've tossed it aside or will shout your name next, and it will be your turn to be questioned by the earnest interpreter. You'll walk down the aisle as slowly as you can. You've never been called on like this before and don't know exactly how to behave. Can you be sure his interpretations will correspond to your answers? He could make up your history for you; word for word will be entirely different from your recitation, and you will never be aware of the discrepancy. What turn would this scenario have taken without the translator? Two men stop to eat cupcakes and drink instant coffee.

Perhaps half the plane is asleep although it's only twilight in whatever city you're in. A vehicle moves closer to the plane, but not for purposes of rescue. The plane is being refueled. Another city must be found. The sign lights up telling you to fasten your seatbelt, and the plane taxis down the runway. The translator hasn't met you yet and, for the time being, your respective fictions remain separate revisions.

On Habit

Rehabilitation

*L*EDA AND THE *Swan,* painted by Correggio, was first sold in Prague during the early 1600s. The original was stolen and subsequently taken to Moscow, but a copy, done while the painting was intact, remained behind. The original picture eventually traveled back to Rome where it was sold, then sold again, finally ending up in the collection of a duc d'Orleans, a man who, after the death of his wife, engaged in a series of obsessive projects with a sense of purpose and entitlement founded in what he passed off as religious rejuvenation. His thoughts about women were eclipsed by the need to reverse those thoughts (persistent demons, embarrassing and out of control) and to destroy any images which hinted at or led to them. Pictures which had been like a perfume to him now made him gag. Within his estate he could do whatever he wanted to, and so the stage on which his madness was acted upon found its limits, its proscenium arch, orchestra pit, cranes and winches within these confines. The objects he'd spent a lifetime collecting were at his disposal. They wouldn't talk back. In his compulsiveness he looked at all illustrations of eroticism, however oblique, as symbols to be obliterated. Even harmless bits and pieces, not overtly erotic or sexual, took on a criminal aura and therefore had to be destroyed. His obsession, a project of negation, targeted lampposts, statues, decorative objects, clay pitchers, soup spoons, but paintings came

under the most excessive scrutiny. During this period he beheaded Correggio's *Leda,* then slashed the canvas into narrow strips, leaving it in a pile with other paintings, drawings, and outstretched marble hands severed in the middle of grasping nothing much at all. Looking = touching he screamed in agony as he smashed hitching posts and cisterns. He also slashed another erotic Correggio, *Io,* but this one was a copy. *Leda,* the one he so desired to castrate, was the original.

Years later someone found the tattered bits and pieces hanging from an old frame, had the surface sewn back together again and the severed head repainted. In 1806 the patched-up painting was stolen by Napoleon, who had the head repainted again. By 1968, when Man Ray's *Object to be Destroyed* had been hacked up and reconstructed as *Indestructible Object,* the head in the surviving Correggio had been repainted four times. The copy made in Prague has survived intact.

Habitual Offenders

PILES OF BODIES were uncovered years after the massacres had taken place. Only body parts remained: limbs frozen in ambiguous gestures, sections of bodies were photographed as they embraced or clung to one another in fear, torsos were found as if they had been told to lie face down on the ground before they were shot. By the time the photograph was taken most visceral organs had been eaten away, some remains could be either male or female, some faces still screamed, some had been burnt off, or sliced to ribbons. Few could be identified. Each photographed figure had been reduced to forensic evidence, a series of clues as to how he or she was killed. Bullet casings found at the site were stamped with the imprint of a manufacturer located in St. Louis, Missouri, an unknown city hundreds of miles to the north. But the nameless bodies were reduced to what hadn't decayed: bones, sometimes skin, clothing. Clothing was important for identifying individuals because a person might have been known to possess only one shirt.

The soldiers who killed at El Mozote killed as part of their daily routine and were convinced that those they didn't kill, regardless of the victim's age, would eventually turn on them.

Habitué

MANY PEOPLE chose to haunt Futurama. After standing in line you would take your place in a high-backed chair which, straight-sided and blinkered, prevented peripheral vision. You were forced to stare directly ahead. Once seated you enjoyed a simulated flight over the projected landscape of 1960. From an aerial perspective you looked down at tiny skyscrapers, interstate highways, city streets lined with glass apartment buildings. Automatons sat behind the wheels of cars shaped like silver hot dogs, and a model of General Motors headquarters, a tiered spaceship, reigned over the utopian landscape. The predicted city of 1960 with its verdant meridians and frozen pedestrians ran smoothly and silently. Nineteen thirty-nine needed the idea of 1960. The Sphere and the pointed Trylon buildings glittering with crypto-Freudian possibilities, Democracity designed by Henry Dreyfuss, the Entertainment Zone, where Chesterfield cigarettes promised "more pleasure from the World of Tomorrow," were popular, but the crowds who flocked to the World's Fair were repeatedly drawn to Futurama. Nineteen thirty-nine was left on the subway, in the parking lot, trapped in a radio turned off before the broadcast began. By day Futurama was cheap-looking. You could see the rivets, the bargain basement construction, and the shoddy paint job, but by night it had an eerie, ethereal quality. Its lights promised a city which never slept, transforming itself into a slightly jazzier, more mysterious, less antiseptic form. On leaving, each person received a pin which read "I Have Seen the Future."

In September 1939, in response to Stalin's invasion of Poland, the lights in the Soviet Pavilion were put out. Illuminated limbs of people standing nearby disappeared in the darkness, and the line of structures which bordered the Lagoon of Nations looked gap-toothed and uncanny. Far away on the other side of the park the habitués of Futurama emerged, fingering their pins, looking for car keys and subway tokens, but the horseshoe-shaped USSR building, sandwiched between Rumania and Czechoslovakia, was, for them, invisible.

Storytown

ALICE FOLLOWED a yellow brick road until it forked. She took the left path which turned into dirt as soon as it curved around a cluster of pine trees. *Employees Only* signs led to a corrugated green plastic shelter containing lockers. The shelter was beginning to feel cold in the morning. Even in late August Alice sometimes felt the edge of frost. Soon Storytown would close, summer workers would go back to school or look for other jobs. She changed into a blue dress, white apron, striped stockings, and a blonde wig. The hair was grayish-blonde, stiff as straw, and damaged in places. Stuffing her own hair under it, she talked to her reflection in the partially de-silvered mirror hanging from one of the corrugated walls. Her face looked distant as if she were standing in another room, and she repeated a few of her lines out loud, practicing rabbit talk because no one was listening.

I'll look first and see whether it's marked poison.

Since June, Alice had worked in the Wonderland section of Storytown holding a rabbit for hours, talking to him, and letting children pet him. She had to converse with the animal as if he were a person who might eventually talk back or at least answer simple questions.

Was I the same when I got up this morning? If not, who am I?

In Wonderland her companions were the shy Drink Me, the Mad Hatter, and the Red Queen, a retired music teacher whose costume looked more like a stack of tires than a chess piece, and the March Hare/White Rabbit, a real animal. She cleaned his pen, fed him, and at the end of the day gently eased him out of his little blue jacket, gold watch painted on. Flinty shreds of white fur clung to her blue dress.

Almost everyone at work had plans that involved leaving town, and by October Alice expected the empty, familiar streets to close in on her as if she had been punished and left behind. The 7-Eleven, the dry cleaners, downtown parking lots covered in snow; all these presented an airless panorama with only a few moving figures left in it. The Sheriff of Nottingham had joined the marines, Captain Hook was leaving for Anaheim and Disneyland, one of the Lost Boys had a job waiting for him in New York, Peter Pan was going to art school. They spoke as if they formed a club of departures with their own language of reservations, packing, and driving away. The Fairy Godmother, a history teacher who had been laid off from the high school, planned to apply for unemployment. Between her weekly appearances to sign for her checks she would drive to the next state and tour colonial houses. There was little work to be found on the lake after September, and though Alice had saved some money to leave town she didn't know what she could do if she traveled someplace else. She made up titles for her occupation, writing *custodial performance artist* when she filled out forms for clerical jobs that would begin in the fall. Her mother, an anesthetist who worked in a small hospital, didn't have many people to put to sleep and often let Alice use the car. She had suggested Alice take classes at night, but after her first days at Storytown, she was too tired from standing and talking all day to drive to the next town to learn word processing or library science. Sometimes she fell asleep after work, or she might drive to the lake and watch the summer people in their white clothes grilling food over mesquite fires.

Taped to her locker was a postcard sent from Darryl, the former Sheriff of Nottingham. If anyone wanted to write to him, the postcard said, he was aboard the USS *Guam* in

Tripoli. In the early part of the summer Alice used to cut through Sherwood Forest to talk to Darryl, and now he was in Lebanon. She had few images of where he was living or stationed, and she hadn't written to him. He was more easily pictured at work and in costume. When they used to drive around together they often passed the missile base on their way up to the lake.

"Maybe they'll make you a guard right here." When Darryl talked about his plans to enlist, Alice thought he'd be stationed in town. It seemed logical and would save the marines transportation costs.

"You need clearance to get in."

Alice remembered the word *clearance.* As he said it he had shifted gears, and she played with the radio. A local announcer recommended Mr. Subb's Triple Decker Three Meat Sandwich. *Mr. Sa-ubb off Route 7.* The ad was followed by the weekend schedule at Lebanon Valley Speedway, a drag strip which locals frequented more often than the horse track. *The Thrills! The Chills!* The dj used an echo chamber. Then the radio played prerecorded announcements. *Be all that you can be.* Darryl sang along in a screechy high register, as if the public service announcement about the army were one of hysteria. At the gate to the base, whose cinder-block buildings were painted the color of sand, was a sentry box. It was always manned, and he spoke of buildings, silent and windowless, set back from the road, as if they were part of another amusement park, one which accepted only certain visitors.

"I don't care whether I'm up the lake or over the ocean."

The Sheriff of Nottingham had been one of the few characters whose costume didn't look ridiculous. Somehow he had talked his way out of having to wear tights. Thin olive trousers made Darryl look more like an Allied pilot just back from bombing targets well into Axis territory. Nobody complained that his costume may not have been historically accurate. He tossed bottles into trash cans which seemed miles away and gave inquiring visitors complicated directions to distant campsites and Iroquois burial mounds on the other side of the lake. In or out of costume, in the parking lot or in town, his indifference as he strolled through Storytown suggested the mission had been accomplished without thinking twice about it. He couldn't care less.

Alice liked driving to the lake with him, putting her bare feet on the dashboard and playing the radio. She could have stayed in the front seat for hours looking out the window in silence as they drove further and further north, but Darryl usually wanted to stop when he saw people he knew, or if he thought he recognized a strand of car lights at a beach or remote lakeside bar. As soon as she saw blinking tavern lights or clusters of glowing cigarettes by the shore Alice wanted to drive quickly on, but they nearly always stopped, Darryl yelling as he slammed out of the car. Alice would pour beer foam into the sand and poke it around with her toes or try to play pool with another woman if they were inside, then as everyone else left, Darryl would drive her home.

Sometimes they found a deserted place to park. The turnoff was badly marked, deliberately hard to find, yellow sign bent as if it had been hit by a truck. If there were a few other cars at one clearing he drove further down the dirt road.

Darryl had spent a lot of time looking for a car without bucket seats and a gearshift stuck in the middle. Finally he located an older car with bench seats which he bought without hesitation even though its body was rusted. The upholstery was blue with silver threads running through it, and the button door locks stood up aggressively at what seemed like about six inches, even when pressed down as far as they would go.

They stayed in the clearing all night, but in the morning it was obvious others had been there. Sites where cars had been parked in the rain were marked by oil slicks which resembled miniature environmental disasters; one kind of microbe floundering in gasoline, another kind eating it up. On the ground were bent cans, beer and Coke, used rubbers, crumpled Marlboro packages. Wet ants swarmed over what looked like a taco rind.

ONE NIGHT they slipped back into Storytown and tried to find a house with a usable bed but all of them were painted props, hard and too small for two people or even one adult, so they slept on the grass near the rabbit hutch. Darryl imitated the manager, Mr. Mink, saying, "With all due respect, no one sleeps in Wonderland. We are awake and alert at all times." Alice propped her feet on a concrete mushroom and laughed at him.

"Sometimes I feel like an imposter," she said.

"You are."

"No, that's not what I mean." She told him about a movie she'd watched late at night, *The Man Who Never Was*, about a body the English army had decided to let the Germans find, giving it a fraudulent identity and planting false war plans on the corpse. The body was dropped into the sea from an airplane, and the Germans picked it up, just as the officers had predicted they would. In an explanatory scene Alice remembered there had been a map with animated arrows and swastikas on it showing the war's progress. A voice supposedly coming over German radio repeated: *Martin genuine, Martin genuine,* again and again. He hadn't been genuine, and the Germans were fooled by this elaborate ruse. Alice tried to explain that she felt like Martin, a plant with a false identity. Before he fell asleep Darryl told her that as he remembered it the English had been on the winning side.

"WHERE'S TRIPOLI?"

"I don't know. They'll put me on a boat. I'll get off the boat. I'll be there."

The animated map went berserk. Arrows and flags bounced in different directions toward its margins. To Darryl all continents were part of Storytown on a global scale. When they walked through Sherwood Forest or Wonderland, he reduced the whole world to something local and understandable, a question of parking problems and where to buy cheap gasoline.

"The marines will ship me down the Hudson, across the Atlantic, through the Strait of Gibraltar, and across the Mediterranean."

"And then where?"

"What difference does it make?"

"The summer is just beginning." She rubbed her ankle where bone knocked against dashboard, then flipped the sun visor to look in the mirror behind it, putting on lipstick by the reflected gleam of headlights from a car behind them. She stuck the cap between her toes.

"There's nothing to do here."

"Don't blame me." Darryl drove through the rain, windshield wipers mimicking a wheezing sound, as if his car lacked the conviction to really go anywhere anyway. The wipers smeared dirt and water into fan shapes.

"Sounds like an asthmatic."

"It's only a car."

Alice opened the window a crack so that the rain hit her face. They were driving past the racetrack. White fence posts, dimly lit from streetlights, looked like drive-in movie speakers in the rain, but there was no movie, only scattered horse vans and boarded-up betting stands.

"There might be an umbrella in the backseat, somewhere under all that junk."

Alice climbed over the seat and rummaged around the old coffee cups and Coke cans. Darryl watched her in the mirror, first her bare feet as she squirmed over the seat, then the top of her head looking around.

"There's nothing here. Who are you going to fight in Lebanon?"

He shrugged, squinting into the rain as another car's headlights appeared from around a curve in the road.

SEE YOUR favorite characters come to life, billboards along the highway read. As a child Alice loved being taken to Storytown. Although she looked forward to each trip, when they actually arrived the park often turned out to be less wonderful than advertised. The man who lifted children onto rides was rough, squeezing their chests as if looking for something, then dropping them into carts or horses like they were sacks of beans. He blatantly checked out her mother. Cinderella pouted even when she was supposed to be on her way to the ball. The ride in the pumpkin coach was monotonous and only brought her back to where she had started. The Prince's castle was a tiny model of molded plastic at the top of an unnaturally symmetrical mountain. Later, in the picnic area, small chairs and tables made of concrete and screwed into the ground were cold in the shade. When Alice thought about it, she realized the stories whose endings she had learned had been reconstructed to be circular. Cinderella went back to her hearth, not a throne, for the next round of visitors who would walk through her story. Snow White became lost again. Sleeping Beauty went back to sleep. Although this had seemed false to Alice, and the repetition of each story subverted its preciousness, she would still go through the stories more than once if she could get away with it. When Cinderella became annoyed after her third time around and told her she should give other children a chance, Alice turned red and stepped away from her mother. Squinting and rubbing her sunglasses on the edge of her plaid shorts, her mother said, Just ignore her, but Alice never went near that part of Storytown until she applied for a job ten years later.

THE MANAGER'S office was in a Dutch cottage with a windmill attached. There was a sign on his desk that read: *Everything has a moral if you can find it. Lewis Carroll.* Alice found the quote staring her in the face during her job interview. She knew the line belonged to the Duchess toward the end of the story when she was being peppery and impossible, but for the manager the saying was a pleasant platitude as useful and as informative as those printed on the complimentary refrigerator magnets her mother received from drug companies advertising anti-depressants and blood coagulants. *A silver lining in a jar.* Alice liked the idea of a promise, of revised expectations, but couldn't herself believe in the magnets. He had asked her if she got along well with the public. While trying to think of who the public might be she remembered the man who handled children before putting them into rides they couldn't extricate themselves from without help. He waited for an answer. She said yeah, all right, and when she and Peter were finally hired Alice thought it was because of their names. She had no qualifications, and in a way felt sorry for Mr. Mink because coincidences mattered to him, as if there might be no other reasonable motive for giving someone a job. Later Alice learned that his reputation as the martinet of Storytown was inconsistent. Mr. Mink chewed gum, carried bags of potato chips that he gave to lost children, and kept a gun in his desk. Drink Me said the gun wasn't real, but Buffalo Bill insisted that it was, and Drink Me wouldn't know the difference anyway. There were occasions, such as the outbursts of Walter Philips, who worked as Captain Hook, when he seemed to have other fish to fry and those other fish made him sad and untalkative. He was so distracted after Darryl left to join the marines the Sheriff was never replaced.

"The summer's been slow on account of the rain," he explained while checking on the rabbit, poking his fingers into the cage to stroke his nose. "People used to leave their kids at Storytown, then go to the track, but even the track's been closed more days this year."

Alice's mother had seen him in the hospital where she worked, occasionally catching a glimpse of him turning a corner or walking slowly down a corridor. Whether he was visiting someone or undergoing some kind of outpatient treatment, her mother didn't know. She had asked Alice if she would like her to find out why he was "in," as her mother would say, but Alice didn't want to know. She didn't like to think of Mr. Mink sitting in his Dutch cottage staring at the empty parking lot, calling the hospital or holding his head in his hands before he cleaned out his desk for the season.

PERCHED ON the edge of Route 9, Storytown verged on north woods that threatened to encroach on its painted borders and absorb its little structures in an overgrowth of pine and sumac. Cars rushed past on their way to Canada, but for Alice, stuck in one spot, the amusement park had the ability to transform itself into a landscape of complete humiliation. The transformation, based on accident, on minutiae, crept up on her. In the middle of the summer her wig blew off, landing in a tulip bed, and not only had dirt clung to the nylon strands, but some kind of gummy candy stuck to the wig as well. Alice rinsed the fake hair off under a drinking fountain and laid it on top of the concrete Walrus. The Carpenter's head was too large. Alice's own hair was brown, curly, and un-Alice-like, so when the wig dried she combed it and put it on again. Walter Philips had noticed the wig on the Walrus and witnessed Alice replacing the thing on her own head. At closing time he walked her to the gate. He was friendly, touching her as if by accident as they walked down the Yellow Brick Road toward the entrance.

"It's not easy being Captain Hook," he said. "Every day I make very small children cry. I'm the bad guy around here."

Alice didn't know what to say. He smelled of chocolate

bars and stale cigarette smoke. He stuffed his hook into the pocket of the red satin costume and rubbed his left hand.

"It gets cramped from having to remain in a sleeve all day. Heard from Darryl lately?"

"No."

Alice almost felt sorry for him. At the entrance to the employee changing rooms, the manager approached. Suddenly Walter screwed his hook into the dangling sleeve and without malice, as if a joke, described the entire incident with the wig to Mr. Mink.

"Her rug landed in a pile of crap, and she washed it off and stuck the thing on the Carpenter. She's a mental case."

"How does it look, Alice, when families visit, what do they see? A blond Walrus." The manager didn't laugh. He seemed preoccupied and, anxious to lock up, said nothing more to her.

Once Walter began there was no stopping him. Doing her job, attempting to speak convincingly to the rabbit or smiling at children, all these job requirements looked ridiculous and Walter, a talented mimic, knew it. He was the feather in the armpit, needing everyone to laugh so he wouldn't be ignored or punched, his matchbook rolling under the coffee machine, his chin hitting linoleum. He soon found other ways of torturing her, like telling all of Wonderland that she had been seen in the Sheriff of Nottingham's car, and they had been speaking to each other in the voices of their characters.

"What a curious feeling. I must be shutting up like a telescope."

He paused, waiting for laughter. It was difficult to know what to do in the face of Walter's fictional impersonation. His narrow eyes and long face conveyed the intense pleasure he got from making the others laugh at someone else's expense. His quickness and desire to mirror the absurdity of Alice's situation defied any attempt to defuse him. Alice actually laughed at his caricatures, but she never said those kinds of things to Darryl. All she did was ride in his car and play with the radio.

"*Dar-ryl!*" Walter trilled.

"Get lost. Go back to Never-Never Land, will ya?" The Mad Hatter fanned his sweating face with his hat, pushing a child away with his free hand.

The Red Queen hummed "Love makes the world go round," a line that actually would have belonged to the bad-tempered Duchess, had she been represented in Wonderland. In the story Alice responded that the world was made to go round by everyone minding their own business, but the Duchess had countered: love and minding your own business were absolutely the same thing. She stayed as far from the Red Queen as possible, pretending the rabbit needed special attention. Darryl was traveling around the world or the world stood still as he pushed onward. She watched the news about Lebanon when it was on television, but the pictures of car bombs and roadblocks went by quickly, and she couldn't picture Darryl in that or any other city.

CARS OF fractious and impatient children were already filling the parking lot as Alice walked past a plot of concrete toadstools with vermilion caps. She took a cigarette out of her apron pocket and cut through Sherwood Forest. She waved to Captain Hook in exile on his island, fanning himself with his big hat and scratching his head under his Dutch Masters Cigar wig. He yelled at her from his minuscule territory.

"No smoking on the premises." Walter made a sweeping gesture with his hook to indicate the lay of the land.

She tossed the cigarette behind a concrete mushroom. Mr. Mink had cut back on the Lost Boys, always in nightshirts. Peter Pan was still on the artificial island, stuck with Walter Philips. Tinkerbell was a puppet operated by Peter Pan himself. Earlier in the summer Peter had worked as Drink Me, the worst job in Storytown. He had to spend the entire day in a hot bottle suit and could sit down only in the employee cafeteria during lunch. In agony he had once pulled his arms into the boxlike suit and sat curled up inside, but that had only made him feel faint and claustrophobic, as if he were submerged at the bottom of the lake. Still, it had been funny the way he made his limbs vanish into the bottle suit. At lunch he drew a picture of himself on a paper napkin, finally giving it to Alice at the end of the day. The drawing looked like an anatomical diagram of Peter crunched into a fetal position inside a cross-section of the bottle. Peter, pale and inky, had been in Alice's class in school, and sometimes she gave him rides home. He rarely said anything.

Toward the end of the summer the atmosphere in the park approached anarchy. A boy in a T-shirt that read *Sick of It All* mimicked her as she spoke, standing right in front of her. The next day a tiny child ran terrified of the March Hare, and the girl's sister yelled at them, tripping over a pop-up sprinkler head during the chase, cutting her knee open. One of the Three Little Pigs greeted a fat man, calling him "Uncle Bob," and the man complained to Mr. Mink. He claimed he thought the man really was a relative; it was hot inside the pig suit, and sweating, he couldn't see very well through the badly aligned eye slits in the pig costume's head.

The manager lectured them on the importance of congeniality and fired the third pig. Storytown closed out the summer with only two. Crack vials and a few used condoms and wrappers were found in the parking lot and behind Snow White's house. Although Darryl was long gone the discovery made Alice feel exposed, as if someone knew what they'd done, then left a trail of clues to show they knew. She looked for video cameras in the eaves.

The incident which caused the greatest ruckus occurred when someone broke into Storytown and painted *U.S. OUT OF LAKE GEORGE* on the side of Cinderella's coach and again on Rapunzel's tower. Alice tried to write to Darryl about the episode but wasn't sure it would be humorous to him. She wasn't sure Darryl would care about Storytown anymore, or how he would feel about slogans he might take personally. After the graffiti episode Mr. Mink tried to increase security in Storytown.

"Only a paranoid," he told the police who came the following day, "would make any connections between an amusement park and the missile base up the lake. Any conspiracists in the mountains this summer? They never target the track." While watching a talk show he had learned about people who believed in vast conspiracy theories which linked disparate elements: pizza franchises, covert arms deals, small airlines, and drug cartels located in cities he couldn't find on a map.

The police were busier during the summer than the rest of the year and couldn't really help Mr. Mink except to offer suggestions about an alarm system.

"We have a real threat here." He offered them potato chips.

"It's probably just summer people." They leaned against their cars and wrote notes.

Alice imagined the vandals returning, wearing ski masks over their heads and carrying an arsenal of spray paint. She would come to work one morning and find evidence of midnight arson: a lurid, bombed-out relic of Cinderella's coach, a burnt Halloween shell; Rapunzel's tower, a spiral skeleton; and windmills lying in pieces among the toadstools. The March Hare would be lost in the forest to the north of Storytown and Buffalo Bill's horse would be found gnawing half-frozen hot dogs, or he might follow a trail of potato chips blowing in the breeze, eddying in drifts down the yellow brick road. But the vandals didn't return. At home her mother watched television news. A car bomb had gone off in a market in Beirut, killing over a dozen people at last count. Their reception was poor, but in the seconds the image flashed on the screen Alice made out a pair of legs sticking out from under part of a car, surrounded by broken glass. Captain Hook, a ninny, not a ninja, seemed small and trite. She put the letter in a book and never mailed it. When talking to the police Mr. Mink had used the word *malign,* but the only malignity Alice could think of was the feet sticking out from under the bombed car like the witch's feet under Dorothy's battered house in *The Wizard of Oz.* As she drove past the guarded buildings set off from the road, she remembered Mr. Mink telling the police that he personally supported the base and did so wholeheartedly.

SHE LIKED being alone in Wonderland, especially in the early morning when dew was still slick on plastic flamingos that were supposed to be Wonderland croquet mallets. Wooden hedgehog balls were screwed into place near playing card arches so they wouldn't be stolen. The tableau looked as if it had been permanently stopped midgame. A pine grove lay on the other side of the park's fence, and Alice used to imagine that the real characters lurked in the dense trees, angry at the way they had been frozen and misrepresented. The summer was nearly over. She began to wear a Walkman under her wig. No one stopped her.

During lunch Peter Pan talked about art school for the first time while Alice shot a stream of Coke into her mouth by putting her thumb over one end of the straw. He wanted to take her picture while she was in costume so she slapped the hot, itchy wig back on her head and looked in a bewildered way at the camera. Everyone was talking in loud voices, acting in character while out of context, mimicking whining children and Mr. Mink.

"*Why is a raven like a writing desk?*" Alice recited lines from the scene of the mad tea party. "*It wasn't very civil of you to sit down without being invited.*" Captain Hook minced past her table, balancing his wig at the end of a rubber sword. She shouted in his direction. "*You should learn not to make personal remarks. It's very rude.*"

"*Congeniality is paramount!*" Peter warned, running his hand through his unwashed hair so that it stood straight up.

In the midst of their hilarity the Red Queen entered the lunchroom red-eyed. Drink Me, swinging his bottle suit by the rim circling the stopper, nearly clobbered her.

"It's the Queen! It's the Queen!" he shouted.

"Drink Me, you're an idiot," she said, rubbing her eyes. Red makeup came off on her hands, and she walked away from him into the middle of the group, then stood very still, looking at them as if they were Martians.

"What did I do?" Drink Me asked.

"People, people," the Queen faltered as if she were addressing a classroom, but their silence stopped her. She could barely get the words out and didn't look at Alice at all. The Queen had been having lunch with Mr. Mink in his office when Darryl's mother called. There had been an accident or an explosion in Tripoli.

"No, not an accident," she suddenly corrected herself, changing the explanation, "a fight or a brawl of some kind. We don't know exactly what happened or how Darryl was involved. I mean, his mother doesn't know or didn't say."

"What kind of fight? Was he fighting with other marines? Did they gang up on him?"

"Why would anyone do that?"

"Because Darryl is an oddball."

"Shut up, Walter."

"It was another car bomb, and they're not telling us."

"Who do you think 'they' is?" The Red Queen glowered.

"How should I know?"

"Darryl is dead," the Red Queen said with a vengeance. She hated all of them.

Walter Philips looked at the ground. Drink Me's eyes bulged from his head as if he'd been punched in the stomach, and Peter Pan turned white. There was an awkward silence for several minutes, which the Red Queen broke nervously.

"Mr. Mink wants to put up a plaque in Darryl's memory in Sherwood Forest." The Red Queen, now agitated and weeping, managed to fill their silence with his ideas. "Mr. Mink thought Darryl was a hero," she almost pleaded with them, as if they were vicious Munchkins and nothing more.

Alice felt as if she were trapped in a telephone booth that turned out not to have any handles on the inside, and she'd no change left. Everyone was looking at her. She walked out of the room and was glad no one followed her. Loose maps of Storytown blew past her as she made her way back to Wonderland. Despite the visits by police, despite his platitudes and frustration, Mr. Mink couldn't put his hands on *malign,* and therefore couldn't identify malignity when it appeared, much less keep it out. He didn't know exactly where Tripoli was either.

"You shouldn't enlist."

Even if she had told him, he would have gone anyway. Darryl's idea of who were miscreants and who minded their own business and what's-it-to-you was a rudimentary one. He had not allowed for gray areas, explanations, mitigating circumstances, history, or the role of the sympathetic witness. The Allied pilot had been shot down after all. A stupid man on an unnamed mission, not in the least effortless or heroic, and that was the really stupid part.

IN HER MOTHER'S small house she had very little privacy, but it was empty when she got home. In the summer when there were accidents and urgent operations to be performed she often got emergency calls. She hadn't told her mother about Darryl. Sometimes it was true when she said she was driving to the lake by herself. Lab coats, starched and white, hung in the closet near the front door. The calendar near the telephone was completely marked up: holidays divided the year and dates when cards should be sent for birthdays and anniversaries. Each square contained some reminder or other so that a day was rarely a complete blank. She suddenly pictured the man who used to check out her mother, then feel up children's chests as if his actions were apparent only to Alice. He must have known neither she nor anyone else would stop him. She wondered what had happened to him. An accident, a kidnaping, a bomb, or a fight, and if a fight, with whom?

Again there were no maps for the experience of his death. If he had been in a car accident or drowned, there were pictures for that kind of death, but for an explosion in a strange city there was nothing. For a fight between Americans cooped up in a boat or a barracks, there was also no image. In the future she was afraid she wouldn't be able to drive past the place where stories came to life, but an alternate route from the house to wherever it was she wanted to go might not exist. It was no longer just a summer job where Robin Hood, Captain Hook, Mr. Mink and his gun and chips, all helplessly roiled around together, no longer the kind of job that was difficult to explain to people without everyone breaking out in laughter and disbelief. Even if she hadn't wanted to repeat the night near the rabbit hutch, hadn't written to Darryl, and almost didn't expect to see him again if he had returned, the Red Queen's halting announcement tampered with any attempts she might make to willfully forget.

She turned on the television but muted the sound. "Darryl genuine, Darryl genuine," she kept repeating, as if the story about his death were a marine fabrication devised for reasons she could neither comprehend nor make up. "Genuine,

genuine," she repeated, terrified that she was not.

Her mother had once told her about a patient who had been deliberately incontinent (her description was full of clinical terms) so people would touch her. No one scolded the woman; they silently changed her sheets and clothing until she was released from the hospital. She was sending false signals like the map with animated arrows moving outward toward its margins. Alice went upstairs to her room. She heard a radio across the street, and the music was so urban it took her a while to focus on where she was: maple trees, lawn, birch, sticky peony bush sick with bugs.

"YOUR MOTHER will find you soon," she said, holding the squirming rabbit in one hand. "If she's still in Sherwood Forest, you can only go on to Wonderland from there." Wonderland was the last stop and a dead end. It wasn't connected to any other part of the park. On closing day, a lost child stayed with Alice most of the afternoon. Her name was Starr Flanders. A smile from the Mad Hatter, toothy and sweaty, sent her running to hide behind Alice.

"Come here, sweetheart," the Red Queen said. "I don't eat little girls."

"*You* shouldn't be here, lady." Starr rolled her eyes. "You belong in *Through the Looking Glass.*"

Although annoyed at the suggestion she was out of story, the Queen offered to go to the cafeteria to get her something to eat.

"Nobody knows where your mother is, dearest," she said as she left.

"She could have retraced her steps backwards from Sherwood Forest all the way to Mr. Mink's office at the entrance, but we'll wait here just in case." Alice let Starr hold the rabbit.

"Quitting time," the Mad Hatter said, looking at his watch. "I'll report a lost child to the manager on my way out."

"It's too early. You can't leave yet."

"The Queen's coming back. I'm out of here." Returning sooner than expected because the restaurant was closing and out of nearly everything, they saw her approach from over a hill. Starr was handed a large paper shopping bag that contained only a bottle of juice and a doughnut. Unable to stop the Hatter's premature departure, the Red Queen walked away in a huff. Others were leaving early too; Alice could see characters walking through the trees. One of the Two Little Pigs carried his head in his arms, and Peter Pan twirled the Tinkerbell puppet as he walked along with Drink Me. The lost girl fed bits of the doughnut to the rabbit.

Starr shivered and asked Alice if they would be locked in at night. Orange juice spilled on the grass. It was nearly closing time, and they were the last people left in Storytown. There was no point in waiting for her mother. She had surely gone back to the office. The manager was probably feeding Starr's mother chips and aphorisms until the police arrived. Alice removed the rabbit's jacket, lifted him by the ears, and dropped him in the shopping bag the Red Queen had brought from the cafeteria. They walked through an empty park toward the highway. It was getting dark early, but as they approached they could see Starr's mother in the parking lot talking to Mr. Mink and a policeman. Starr ran ahead of Alice. The manager pointed to them, looking frustrated and painfully aware that he was useless.

"Why didn't you report a lost child?" He had already shuttered his office.

"The Hatter was supposed to tell you."

"I haven't seen any of you Wonderland people since this morning. The Hatter's disappeared."

"Do you want to report another disappearance?" asked the policeman. Alice could see them all reflected in his glasses as if characters lined up to take a bow before a curtain of pine trees. His radio crackled, and he leaned into his car to pick up the receiver.

Mr. Mink shook his head and explained that they were closing up. "I'll be damned if I'll hire that boy again," he said as the police drove away.

Walking across the parking lot, she realized she didn't want to change in the empty corrugated hut with Darryl's postcard still taped to her locker. Everyone had left. She would take her clothes off and sit on the bench, staring at the blotches of sunlight that still mottled the corrugated siding, staring without looking at a postcard of a bazaar in Beirut. Alice folded over the top of the shopping bag and put it in her mother's car. The rabbit, an old and sleepy animal, trembled but remained still in the backseat.

On her way home she stopped by the side of the road and took the rabbit out of the bag. As if terrified or sick, it wouldn't hop away into the woods. She gave him a little nudge, and he appeared to nibble some grass but still wouldn't move. Alice got into the car and drove down the road to an ice cream stand. For a few minutes she stared at the revolving pink and white cone whose lights had just come on, then drove back to where she had left the rabbit. He was still there. Alice lifted him by the ears and put him back in the car. *Kill the wabbit, kill the wabbit,* she suddenly re-membered the Mad Hatter lisping as if he were Elmer Fudd humming "Wabbit Erdamerung" from *What's Opera, Doc?* Alice didn't want to keep the animal, but felt unable to re-turn him to Storytown, which would have been closed any-way. She had no idea what to do with the white rabbit. As she drove toward town she wondered what happened to the animals during the winter. They were probably boarded somewhere. "What difference did it make?" she said out loud. Mr. Mink might rent out the horses and pony. He could buy a new rabbit. They didn't cost that much, she was certain.

He would eventually call her, asking what had happened to the March Hare. *Let me try to remember. I think Hook took him, or it might have been Drink Me.* He wouldn't believe her and at the end of the conversation he would tell her she shouldn't think about working in Storytown again. Her mother, looking up from a medical magazine, might ask who had called and she would answer, oh, just no one.

SHE SHOVED her costume into the incinerator in the backyard, watching the wig melt, as if its melting marked the end of a season of dizziness and puzzlement.

Silence in the court. One of the rabbit's lines that had no place in the Storytown version kept ringing in her head. Mr. Mink had deleted the troubling parts of the original. When Alice said "Stupid things," the animal and bird jurors wrote *stupid things* on their slates. She looked into the incinerator and remembered lines that hadn't been part of the Storytown script: *"You can't behead a head unless there's a body to cut it off from," says the executioner. The King says anything with a head can be beheaded. The Queen will have everyone executed no matter what.*

She sat on the backyard concrete steps hugging her knees until the shadows swallowed her, waiting to grow larger and larger to tower over the town itself as well as Storytown, to be attacked by playing cards which would turn into leaves as she woke up to find that either she had shrunk or everything had grown along with her while she wasn't paying attention.

Alice walked back to the incinerator to be sure it was off, kicking a pile of grass cuttings beside it. Something scurried out from under the damp green pile. Beams from a neighbor's car lights swung round in a curve, catching her as she walked back to the house, a frozen tableau as she reached for the screen door and the face of the white rabbit behind it.

DALKEY ARCHIVE PAPERBACKS

FICTION: AMERICAN

BARNES, DJUNA. *Ladies Almanack*	9.95
BARNES, DJUNA. *Ryder*	11.95
BARTH, JOHN. *LETTERS*	14.95
BARTH, JOHN. *Sabbatical*	12.95
CHARYN, JEROME. *The Tar Baby*	10.95
COOVER, ROBERT. *A Night at the Movies*	9.95
CRAWFORD, STANLEY. *Some Instructions*	11.95
DAITCH, SUSAN. *Storytown*	12.95
DOWELL, COLEMAN. *Island People*	12.95
DOWELL, COLEMAN. *Too Much Flesh and Jabez*	9.95
DUCORNET, RIKKI. *The Fountains of Neptune*	10.95
DUCORNET, RIKKI. *The Jade Cabinet*	9.95
DUCORNET, RIKKI. *Phosphor in Dreamland*	12.95
DUCORNET, RIKKI. *The Stain*	11.95
FAIRBANKS, LAUREN. *Sister Carrie*	10.95
GASS, WILLIAM H. *Willie Masters' Lonesome Wife*	9.95
GORDON, KAREN ELIZABETH. *The Red Shoes*	12.95
KURYLUK, EWA. *Century 21*	12.95
MARKSON, DAVID. *Springer's Progress*	9.95
MARKSON, DAVID. *Wittgenstein's Mistress*	11.95
MASO, CAROLE. *AVA*	12.95
McELROY, JOSEPH. *Women and Men*	15.95
MERRILL, JAMES. *The (Diblos) Notebook*	9.95
NOLLEDO, WILFRIDO D. *But for the Lovers*	12.95
SEESE, JUNE AKERS. *Is This What Other Women Feel Too?*	9.95
SEESE, JUNE AKERS. *What Waiting Really Means*	7.95
SORRENTINO, GILBERT. *Aberration of Starlight*	9.95
SORRENTINO, GILBERT. *Imaginative Qualities of Actual Things*	11.95
SORRENTINO, GILBERT. *Mulligan Stew*	13.95
SORRENTINO, GILBERT. *Splendide-Hôtel*	5.95
SORRENTINO, GILBERT. *Steelwork*	9.95
SORRENTINO, GILBERT. *Under the Shadow*	9.95
STEIN, GERTRUDE. *The Making of Americans*	16.95
STEIN, GERTRUDE. *A Novel of Thank You*	9.95

DALKEY ARCHIVE PAPERBACKS

STEPHENS, MICHAEL. *Season at Coole*   7.95
WOOLF, DOUGLAS. *Wall to Wall*   7.95
YOUNG, MARGUERITE. *Miss MacIntosh, My Darling*   2-vol. set, 30.00
ZUKOFSKY, LOUIS. *Collected Fiction*   9.95

FICTION: BRITISH

BROOKE-ROSE, CHRISTINE. *Amalgamemnon*   9.95
CHARTERIS, HUGO. *The Tide Is Right*   9.95
FIRBANK, RONALD. *Complete Short Stories*   9.95
GALLOWAY, JANICE. *Foreign Parts*   12.95
GALLOWAY, JANICE. *The Trick Is to Keep Breathing*   11.95
MOSLEY, NICHOLAS. *Accident*   9.95
MOSLEY, NICHOLAS. *Impossible Object*   9.95
MOSLEY, NICHOLAS. *Judith*   10.95
MOSLEY, NICHOLAS. *Natalie Natalia*   12.95

FICTION: FRENCH

BUTOR, MICHEL. *Portrait of the Artist as a Young Ape*   10.95
CREVEL, RENÉ. *Putting My Foot in It*   9.95
ERNAUX, ANNIE. *Cleaned Out*   9.95
GRAINVILLE, PATRICK. *The Cave of Heaven*   10.95
NAVARRE, YVES. *Our Share of Time*   9.95
QUENEAU, RAYMOND. *The Last Days*   9.95
QUENEAU, RAYMOND. *Pierrot Mon Ami*   9.95
ROUBAUD, JACQUES. *The Great Fire of London*   12.95
ROUBAUD, JACQUES. *The Plurality of Worlds of Lewis*   9.95
ROUBAUD, JACQUES. *The Princess Hoppy*   9.95
SIMON, CLAUDE. *The Invitation*   9.95

FICTION: GERMAN

SCHMIDT, ARNO. *Nobodaddy's Children*   13.95

FICTION: IRISH

CUSACK, RALPH. *Cadenza*   7.95
MAC LOCHLAINN, ALF. *The Corpus in the Library*   11.95

DALKEY ARCHIVE PAPERBACKS

MacLochlainn, Alf. *Out of Focus*	5.95
O'Brien, Flann. *The Dalkey Archive*	9.95
O'Brien, Flann. *The Hard Life*	9.95
O'Brien, Flann. *The Poor Mouth*	10.95

FICTION: LATIN AMERICAN and SPANISH

Campos, Julieta. *The Fear of Losing Eurydice*	8.95
Lins, Osman. *The Queen of the Prisons of Greece*	12.95
Paso, Fernando del. *Palinuro of Mexico*	14.95
Sarduy, Severo. *Cobra* and *Maitreya*	13.95
Tusquets, Esther. *Stranded*	9.95
Valenzuela, Luisa. *He Who Searches*	8.00

POETRY

Ansen, Alan. *Contact Highs: Selected Poems 1957-1987*	11.95
Burns, Gerald. *Shorter Poems*	9.95
Fairbanks, Lauren. *Muzzle Thyself*	9.95
Giscombe, C. S. *Here*	9.95
Markson, David. *Collected Poems*	9.95
Theroux, Alexander. *The Lollipop Trollops*	10.95

NONFICTION

Ford, Ford Madox. *The March of Literature*	16.95
Green, Geoffrey, et al. *The Vineland Papers*	14.95
Mathews, Harry. *20 Lines a Day*	8.95
Roudiez, Leon S. *French Fiction Revisited*	14.95
Shklovsky, Viktor. *Theory of Prose*	14.95
West, Paul. *Words for a Deaf Daughter* and *Gala*	12.95
Young, Marguerite. *Angel in the Forest*	13.95